THE LIFE OF

CHARLOTTE DYMOND

THE LIFE OF

CHARLOTTE DYMOND

By

Jill Batters

Best Wishes

Jill Batters.

This novel is based on the true facts of a famous
Victorian Cornish murder to which certain names,
characters
and incidents have been added from the author's
imagination.
Apart from the true facts, any resemblance to actual
persons, living or dead, events or localities is entirely
coincidental.

Published by: CB Productions (Cornwall)

Printed and bound by
TJ International of Padstow, Cornwall.

Cover photography and design by
Aidan Booth

ISBN – 978-0-9569189-2-5

This book is dedicated to my
husband Chris for his continual
encouragement and assistance.

By the same author & publisher

From the Vision to the Noose

*A true 1840's Cornish story of
murder and intrigue.*

ISBN 978-0-9569189-0-1

From the same publisher

Marbal House

A house of intrigue, secrets and passion.

ISBN 978-0-9569189-1-8

...Places in the story...

To Launceston

To Altarnun

To ...eston

HALWORTHY

Rosebenault

Trevilian Gate

Tremail chapel

Penhale Farm

To Trespatrett

Higher Down Gate

Halset

Treslay

Davidstow Church

Camelford

To Delabole

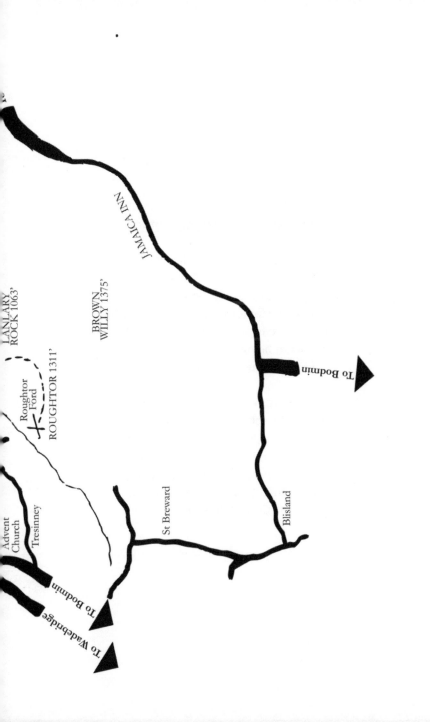

<u>Jill Batters – Cornish Author</u>

Jill Batters is a Cornish writer living in Bodmin,
who launched her first book in 2011,
'From the Vision to the Noose', telling the
story behind a famous Victorian murder that
took place in north Cornwall in 1840,
the victim being the great-grandfather
of the famous novelist Nevil Shute.

Following on from the success of her first book,
'The Life of Charlotte Dymond' tells the story of
yet another well-known Victorian murder,
this time set on Bodmin Moor in 1844. Such
was the mystery and intrigue surrounding this
story that it has become a part of
Cornish folklore.

September 1837

It was a magnificent sight. He always came here to the inn when his people made camp near Trevalga in the summer. Leaning lazily in the doorway; ale in hand, he was captivated once more by the sight of horses and wagons in a line that stretched away from the inn and along the road as far as his eyes could see. And whilst some of the drivers took refreshment inside, the air outside was filled with the noise made by busy blacksmiths and carpenters. The local tradesmen were needed to attend to horses whose shoes had been lost, or to carts and wagons in need of repair during their long journey to and fro from Boscastle harbour. These horses, two or three to a wagon, were on their way back to the harbour with slate from Delabole quarry. Once there, wagons and carts would be loaded with cargo from visiting ships. Precious cargo of coal, iron, salt and timber would be dropped off at various destinations as they made their way back to Delabole slate quarry for the next load. He loved this north coast of Cornwall. It was wild, unpredictable, and dangerous; a lot like his own way of life.

The day was warm, his glass was empty and he was about to turn back into the inn to be entertained for a while by tales of shipwrecks and smuggling, when he noticed a small girl walking fearlessly amongst the powerful, restless horses, apparently as captivated as he was by the sights, sounds and wonder of the day. Struck by her likeness to his own daughter, he watched her as she chatted away to one of the blacksmiths. The likeness was amazing. The dark curls bobbing around as she spoke, the flashing blue eyes in a perfect heart shaped face. But it wasn't just

9

her looks. It was the way she moved, swayed as she talked, waved her arms around and tilted her head when she laughed.

Leaving his empty glass in the doorway, he strolled over to the pair and spoke at first to the blacksmith; he didn't want to startle the child. "That's as fine a pair of horses as I've seen in a while."

The other man eyed him suspiciously. It was the girl who answered him, not seeming to notice his strange accent and clothes. "They are beautiful," she sighed, "Just beautiful."

He smiled at her. "I have horses of my own," he said, "but not like these. Mine are lighter smaller horses that I breed to sell to the gentry. They pay me high prices for a matching team to pull their coaches."

She was listening to him, intrigued by the warm lilt of his voice, when an uneasy horse suddenly swung sideways and knocked her towards the blacksmith. Unfazed, she caught hold of its mane to steady herself.

"Well, you're not afraid of the horses young lady. Used to them are you?" She nodded. He looked around. "Is your father working here?"

"No sir," she smiled, noticing the admiration in his eyes. "I'm here with my mother. My grandmother works in the inn, and we're visiting her. We live at Tresparrett Post."

"And have you got your own horse at Tresparrett Post?"

"No sir, but I have friends who live on a farm. I ride their horses."

"My daughter, she's a little younger than you; has a large fox coloured Shetland pony with a white mane and tail."

10

"What's your daughter's name sir?"

"We named her Unity. Unity Kircher."

"I'm Charlotte, sir. Charlotte Dymond."

"Dymond? That's a pretty name. I knew a girl once by the name of Dymond; Mary Dymond."

"But that's my mother's name sir, Mary Dymond."

"Is that right now? Well I wonder if she's my Mary? Would she be inside the inn Charlotte? I was about to fill up my glass."

"She'll be behind the bar sir. She always helps out when we're here."

Inside the inn it was dark and the air was heavy with tobacco smoke, but he spotted her straight away. She stood with her back to him, fair hair swept up away from her slender neck, chiding some impatient customers as she mopped up spillage behind the bar.

"Just give me a minute. What's the matter with you today?"

"Well now Mary Pleace Dymond. Here we are again then."

She turned to face him, obviously startled. No-one called her Mary Pleace. No-one used her middle name except her James. And then as recognition dawned, her already flushed cheeks turned scarlet.

"Ben," She managed somehow to say his name. "Ben. What are you doing here?"

"Just stopping by for an ale Mary, but I met up with your daughter outside there. She told me her name and that her mother was working inside here."

"Charlotte? I've told that girl not to talk to strangers!"

"Well I'm hardly a stranger am I now Mary?" he interrupted her, smiling. "In fact, now that I've met her, I think there's something you may want to tell me."

11

"And what can I possibly have to tell you Ben Kircher? It's been eleven long years since I last set eyes on you!"

"I thought we might just talk about Charlotte. I have a daughter of my own, so much like her they could be sisters."

"Well my child is nothing to do with you, so you'd do well to get that idea out of your head and go about your own business."

Mary's head was reeling. Just seeing him again had knocked the breath out of her body but she could see determination in his eyes; he wasn't going to let this rest. She knew what she had to do.

"Joseph!" she called to the innkeeper. "I'll just be outside. I need some air."

Leading the way to the little garden at the back of the inn, away from prying eyes, Mary turned to face the man who'd been in her prayers many times over the past eleven years. Prayers that had asked that she might never see him again. Prayers that hadn't been answered!

Charlotte had lost interest now in the horses and was watching the doorway to the inn intently. Who was that strange, dark haired man who said he knew her mother? She couldn't remember ever having seen him before. The noise from the blacksmith's anvil rang loudly in her ears; flies, attracted by the horses in the heat of the day, buzzed around her face, and her view of the entrance was often blocked by the to-ing and fro-ing of the thirsty men folk, but Charlotte, undeterred kept watch for her mother and the man. And then she spotted them, moving quickly and disappearing around to the side of the inn. Gathering up her skirts and running as quickly as her tight little boots would allow, she followed after them.

The blacksmith watched the child scuttle away with amusement. She was far too clever for her own good that one. Her grandmother lived and worked at the inn, and as he lived in one of the few nearby cottages he knew her family well. A friendly little girl, and as pretty as a picture, but far too clever for her own good.

Charlotte ran to the side of the inn, but stopped dead in her tracks when she heard her mother's raised voice. Edging her way into a position where she couldn't be seen, but could clearly hear what was being said, she crouched down out of sight.

The man was speaking now and holding her mother by her arms.

"I'm sure I am that child's father Mary. What have you to say to that? How old is she? If she is mine she should be ten years old now, eleven soon. When was she born?"

"My daughter is only nine years old Ben. Her birthday is very soon right enough, but she will be ten then, not eleven."

Charlotte could not believe her own ears. What was her mother saying? She had turned ten on her last birthday, almost a year since, and would be eleven years old in just a few more days. Unable to watch her mother's distress for another moment, Charlotte carefully crept backwards for several paces and then started to run again, gathering speed as quickly as she could, just as if she had never stopped for a single moment to listen in on their conversation.

"So here you are mother!" She arrived beside them, seemingly concerned and breathless.

"Old Tom said he'd seen you come back here".

"Well Charlotte," the man was looking very pleased to see her. "Your mother's been telling me that it is your birthday soon. So how old will you be then child?"

"I'll be ten sir. Double figures!" and Charlotte, smiling at him, lovingly linked arms with her mother.

"Well now ladies," he paused for a moment, just looking at them both and Charlotte was sure she could see laughter in his eyes.

"I always say I know a good team when I see one! There's nothing more to say for now then. Look after her for me Mary. I'll be back some day." And then he was going; striding off around the side of the inn and out of sight, leaving Mary to stand and stare at her daughter in disbelief, and Charlotte with a hundred questions on the tip of her tongue.

For Mary, the long journey home with the pony and trap they had borrowed for the day, was a difficult one. At first the child chattered on and on about the strange man and his horses, and the fact that his daughter had her own beautiful fox coloured pony with a white mane and tail. They'd seen horses like that she reminded her mother, when a company of travelling actors and horse riders had come to Boscastle. That had been so exciting! But then came the questions.

"What did he mean mother? Look after her for me! He said that he thought he was my father. Is he my father?"

So her daughter had been eavesdropping at the side of the inn! How much had she heard? How could she explain all of this away? She needed an answer quickly and there was only one explanation that might make some sense to the child.

"No Charlotte, you're mistaken child. His accent is strange. You didn't hear him right, that's all. But I did know him before you were born. He's a gypsy Charlotte; a travelling man. He wanted to buy you from me; give me money for my own daughter and take you travelling with him. It seems that his daughter has no other young people for company. He was telling me, when you came running around to us, that he would be like a father to you. I was very angry with him. He spoke as if you were a pony that he could just pay for and take away with him! I don't want you to tell anyone about this Charlotte. Your father would be very upset. You must promise me that you will never repeat a word of it."

Charlotte promised, but she couldn't understand why her mother was saying these things. She knew that children were sometimes sold when their families had no money. There had been a little boy in the village whose father had died in a mining accident. His mother couldn't afford to keep her family anymore, and she had sold him to a rich landowner who had no children of his own. But all of this made no sense at all. She knew what she had heard that day. Her mother wasn't telling her the truth. Silence fell between them and Charlotte, wrapping her shawl around her shoulders against the chill of the night air, comforted herself with the thought that she now had two fathers. One was the butcher from Poundstock, and one was a gypsy man who bred horses for the gentry and had a daughter, her half-sister, who rode a beautiful pony with a flowing white mane and tail.

Mary couldn't sleep that night. Charlotte's words echoed around in her head, forcing her to re-live a day from a very different time in her life, and to see it now in a new light.

15

"Is he my father?
Why did he ask you to look after me for him?
He said he was sure he was my father!"

The truth was that she didn't know. She had, until now, believed that James Medland was Charlotte's father. She even had his colouring, the dark hair and bright blue eyes.

"My little Cornish maid" he called her, on the rare occasions that he did see her. He usually visited when Charlotte was asleep, secret meetings, late on dark evenings, too late for neighbours to unexpectedly call around. Most people knew of course, but little was said, either to her or to Charlotte. She'd been seventeen when he'd first walked into the inn where she'd lived and worked.

"Who's the young woman?" she'd heard him ask Joseph the landlord, and she'd been James' woman ever since. It turned out that he was twenty years older than her and a well to do butcher from Poundstock. She hadn't known at first that he was married with two daughters, Margaret and Elizabeth, who were helping him to look after their ailing mother, Judith. And when she had found him out? Well, it was too late. It was James that she wanted, for as long as he wanted her.

Fourteen years had passed since then, and almost twelve years had passed since that day in early January 1826, when she had travelled to Newquay with her mother Bess to visit their dearest friends Ellen and her husband Richard. Ellen had written a letter begging them to come and see Richard. He was dying she had said, and asking to see them. His last fishing trip had been too much of a strain on him. He had suffered a stroke whilst still out at sea and was now fast fading away. Bess had been distraught and hurriedly made plans for herself and Mary to spend a few days with their old friends. What she hadn't realised though was that this was the last thing on earth that Mary wanted to do. Of course she loved Ellen and of course she wanted to see Richard again before he died, but she also loved James Medland and she wanted so desperately to see him that she didn't want to leave the inn for one minute, just in case he called in and wanted to see her. They'd been together by then for two years, and he had solemnly promised her that one day they would be living together as man and wife and maybe raising their own family. But then, just a week before she had heard the news of Richard's illness, she had broken the news to James that she thought that she was expecting his baby. James had reacted badly.

"You can't be sure yet Mary, don't panic so," he'd told her. "We'll talk about it another day. I have to go home now to Judith. She's taken a turn for the worse and the girls are worried." And planting a hurried kiss on her cheek he had walked out of the inn, and she hadn't seen him or heard anything more from him since then. No, she definitely did not want to go to visit Ellen and Richard at that time. Nevertheless her conscience wouldn't let her stay away. Her whole family owed that dear couple so much.

Bess and Ellen had first met when they were small orphans living in the workhouse at St Columb Major. Their life had been hard with little time for childish things, but they had at least been given instruction in both reading and writing. Bright, hard-working and eager to learn, they became almost inseparable and believed that fortune had at last smiled on them, when they were taken on together to work as servants in the kitchen at Poldune Manor house near Newquay.

As time passed by though, their lives were to take very different directions. Ellen, who had grown to be a fine and strong young woman, met and married Richard, an older but prosperous fisherman from Crantock, and over time she gave birth to five healthy and hardy sons. Bess however, had not been quite so fortunate. Pretty, dainty and fun loving, she had caught the eye of her master's second son, John. Sir William Burnard's second son was a somewhat simple, but womanising young man, and so, just a few months later, Bess, predictably, found that she was expecting his child. In quick succession she had lost her virginity, her work at the manor as a kitchen maid, and, of course, her home. But Ellen and Richard, hearing of her plight, had come to her rescue, taken her in and cared for her, before, during and after the birth of baby Luke. Fortune had smiled on Bess once more when Richard's close friend, Joseph Luxon, the landlord of the Trevalga Inn, about twenty miles up the coast near Boscastle, in the parish of Trevalga, had offered her work and a new home at the inn. Joseph and Hester his wife had been married for ten years but were still childless. The opportunity to employ Bess to work in the bar and the kitchen whilst they helped to look after baby Luke, had been for them a dream come true. And Bess, secure in the knowledge that she could stay there with them for as long as she needed to, went on, over time, to fill their loving arms with two more fatherless little babies in Thomas and Mary. And so Mary and her brothers had grown up in a small hamlet on the north coast of Cornwall and learned to love its beautiful, if stormy and dangerous coastline. Bess and Ellen had remained the best of friends, exchanging lengthy letters and visiting each other at least once a year.

Earlier in the same year that Richard suffered his stroke, he had moved away from Crantock with his family, and settled in a comfortable cottage very near to the coast in Newquay. With five strapping boys about the place, their home was usually full of noise and laughter. On that sad day in early December though, the atmosphere in the cottage was sombre. The boys had all gone out, and while Richard lay helpless upstairs in bed, Bess and Mary had sat in the kitchen sorrowing over the wretched condition of a man they loved like a favourite uncle. Ellen though, had seemed to sense that Mary's almost hysterical tears were for more than the shock of seeing Richard struck down in this way, and, taking pity on the girl, had suggested that she took a walk to the beach to calm herself down.

"Take Sebby with you Mary," she'd said. "He loves it down on the beach." Sebby was Ellen's large and clumsy dog who had proved very eager to accompany Mary on her walk. It was a bright and clear day but a strong wind blew Mary's hair into her eyes, making progress slow. Sebby'd raced ahead, his high spirits whipped into a frenzy of excitement, and Mary soon realised that he was leading her, not to the beach, but up onto the rough field on the edge of a line of cliffs, which jutted out far into the sea. The stormy conditions were having an equally strong effect on her own low spirits, releasing the bottled up anger and disappointment that she had felt since breaking the news of the baby to James. Where was he? She'd longed for the comfort of his arms; longed to hear his voice telling her that everything would be alright. From somewhere through the howling wind she'd heard Sebby bark. She had lost sight of him. Frantically she'd looked around, seeing for the first time the

19

angry sea, the huge waves lashing the rocks and then, the strangest sight of all; a young man; running towards her, waving his arms, shouting something that she couldn't hear above the wind. It was then that she'd felt a massive blow from the side, knocking her off balance, pushing her towards the edge of the cliff. She was falling, grabbing rocks, clutching at grass, but just as she'd disappeared over the edge she'd felt herself being pulled back. Grabbed by her skirts, she was thrown to the ground and dragged backwards to the safety of the rough field. He had saved her. The young man who had been hurtling towards her, shouting and waving his arms, was lying on the ground beside her. He had saved her.

"That dog could have killed you! You were too close to the edge!" He'd sounded angry. So it was Sebby who had jumped up and hit her in the side, almost pushing her off the cliff top to be smashed against the rocks below.

The man had rolled away from her and was sitting up, rubbing his legs and knees. She had tried to scramble to her feet but she'd started to tremble and felt light headed. Her boots had caught in her long skirt and she'd stumbled, but in her struggle to stand upright, the blood had seemed to drain away inside her head and she'd fallen once more to the ground in a dead faint.

"Where am I?" She'd opened her eyes and realised that they were inside; shut away from the elements in a small, stone built room. She was lying on the floor on a rough blanket, with Sebby curled up beside her fast asleep. The man was crouching in front of a small open fireplace, kindling a fire from some of the straw and wood that was stored against the wall.

"We're in the huer's hut. Lie still, it will warm up soon."

The huer's hut. The little house right at the end of the bay that was manned in the summer by the men they called 'huers', watching out for the massive shoals of pilchards that would swim in, too close to the shore. These were the men that would first alarm the local fishermen, and then guide their boats to the shoals using semaphore, to show them where to throw their nets. The fishermen of Crantock and Newquay owed much of their prosperity to the pilchard fishing. But the work was gruelling and often exhausted the men and indeed the women who helped to bring the fish ashore.

"What am I doing in here? I must take Sebby home. He's not my dog." The man had moved across to sit beside her.

"Shush woman, you're not well enough to walk home yet and I'm not carrying you again. I don't know how I got you here at all with that dog bouncing around me!"

The anger had gone from his voice but she was finding it hard to understand him. His accent was strange to her and then she realised that he was not from these parts; he was a travelling man, a gypsy. He must have seen the sudden fear in her eyes for he'd said "I won't hurt you," and a little bubble of hysteria had welled up inside so that she'd started to laugh.

"I know," she'd said "You saved my life."

And then they were both laughing and looking straight into each other's eyes. She was looking at him properly for the first time. Not much older than her, she thought, with roguish blue eyes and a bewitching smile. He had saved her and she was feeling so lucky just to be alive.

"I can't bear to think about what would have happened to me if you hadn't been here today," she'd said. "What brought you up here walking alone along the cliff top?"

"I was born in Cornwall," he said "just outside of Helston. We don't come back here very often, but when we do I spend as much time as I can near the sea. I love it; watching the waves, tasting the salt in the air, walking on the cliff tops or on the soft sand. I think the beaches here are the best in the country."

He'd told her his name, Ben Kircher, and that he lived with a group of travelling gypsies who'd been camping in tents outside the town for some weeks. They made baskets and lace for the women to sell in the towns, but mostly they were horse dealers, breeding and selling horses as they travelled around the country. He was moving on early the next morning. His people were ready to travel up through Cornwall again and then further on, possibly as far as Scotland this time.

They had laughed and talked for what felt like hours and she was so relaxed in his company that she'd told him about her family, her life at Trevalga Inn and even her full name, Mary Pleace Dymond.

Hester Luxon, the woman who'd been like a second mother to her, had been Hester Pleace before she'd married Joseph, and as she'd had no daughters of her own, she had wanted Mary named after her. She hadn't told him about James though or the baby. That part of her life was hers and hers alone.

Ben had teased her. "Mary Pleace! It sounds like Mary please." He'd laughed and repeated it. "Mary please, Mary please."

"Please what Ben?" she asked him. "What do you want?"

"Oh let's see. What about a kiss? Just one kiss for saving your life."

She'd moved closer and kissed him hard on the lips.

"Thank you," she'd whispered softly. "Thank you for saving my life." And he'd kissed her back. A warm passionate kiss that had made her long for more. As the warmth was creeping back into her body she'd felt light headed again, giddy, but this time with a strange sense of happiness. All her senses were alive. She could feel the roughness of his skin on her cheek, see arousal in his eyes, smell the sweet scent of wood smoke on his coat. But he'd broken away from her. Surprised, she'd seen that the rogue had returned to his eyes and a little smile played around his mouth.

"So what happens now?" he'd asked, "I could make love to you, but not every woman will let me, even after I've saved her life."

"Oh, and how many women's lives have you saved may I ask?"

She'd sensed that he was testing her, not knowing how she really felt.

"At least one a week," he'd grinned at her. "It's what I do. Walk around on cliff tops waiting for some young lady's dog to try to push them over the edge."

He'd been so full of fun, so carefree; adorable. And so unlike James, who'd always seemed to carry all of his problems like a weight upon his shoulders. But James was twenty years older than this young desirable man. She shivered, wondering what life would do to them in the next twenty years.

"Are you still cold? I can soon warm you up." He'd leaned forward to kiss her again, but as one hand slid around her back, the other began to slowly unbutton the top of her dress.

"Well I'm not going to 'let' you make love to me," she'd said. "I want you to make love to me."

23

"Be sure now," he'd warned, his smile broadening, "I won't be here tomorrow and I can't take you with me. My women folk would surely tear you apart. I suppose I could hide you in one of the carts, cover you over with blankets and clothes and just bring you out at night to feed you and let you share my bed."

She had raised her arm to hit him, but he'd just kissed her playfully and continued, a little faster this time, with the job of undoing her buttons.
She wasn't ashamed of what had followed. She knew that her passion had been fuelled at first by her continuing anguish over James' silence and the shock of almost dying out there on the rocks below the cliff top. But all that had just melted away as they made love, cocooned in the huer's hut, warmed by his fire, cushioned by her own voluminous skirts and Ben's long coat.

That night, tucked up safely in a little makeshift bed in Ellen and Richard's cottage, she'd felt steady again, her world had stopped spinning, she'd known that everything would be alright. She had a loving family, good friends. They would all help her. James would help her. Now she was just desperate to see him again and she was filled somehow with a new strength and energy. Ben had saved her life and she would always love him for that. She'd fallen under his spell for a while, but, she'd asked herself, what manner of harm could come from such a brief encounter? She was pregnant already, wasn't she?

James had, after all, stood by her. When she arrived back at Trevalga Inn just two days later, she learned that he had been there and had wanted to see her. Later that evening he'd called in again, full of

24

apologies for his behaviour on the day they'd last parted company. He'd been shocked by her news of the baby; worried by the consequences of fathering an illegitimate child. He'd said that while he still loved his wife and daughters and couldn't leave them at that time, he had now made plans for Mary and their child. He had found her a small cottage near the coast at Tresparret Post, which was much nearer to his home at Poundstock. If she agreed, he would support her, pay the rent on the cottage, and they would be able to be together more often, in their own home. He'd even made plans for Mary to earn a little money for herself. Knowing that Bess had taught her to read and write, he'd suggested that she could share that knowledge and set up a little school at the cottage, to teach the children of her neighbours and maybe even those from nearby farms.

Mary, beside herself with joy and relief, had of course agreed. Things had moved quickly after that and when Charlotte was born James had been delighted. Up until that time all the women in his life had had fair hair, Judith, his older daughters and indeed, Mary.
His new baby daughter, like himself, had dark curly hair and deep blue eyes. At last there was someone in his family who looked just like him.

1838 – Mid June – early September

Almost a year passed by before the fateful knock on the kitchen door that was to change all of their lives forever. Mary was teaching some of the neighbours children in the front parlour while Charlotte was washing clothes at the sink in the little kitchen at the back of the cottage. She noticed three strangers, all women, pass slowly by the window; gypsies she'd thought, all wearing headscarves and carrying woven baskets. Quickly wiping her soapy hands on her apron, she crossed the floor and warily opened just the top half of their stable type door. Charlotte smiled at them nervously but they were just staring at her, suspicious sharp eyes in brown weathered faces.

"Would you like some lace miss? Is your mother in?" The oldest woman spoke softly but Charlotte found herself tongue-tied; mesmerized by those brown and unsmiling faces.

"Who is it Charlotte?" Mary's appearance beside her broke the spell, but as the child glanced up at her mother, she saw the colour drain from her face until it was almost as white as the chalk she still held in her hand.

"Lace. We'll have some lace. Ribbons for your hair Charlotte. I'll fetch some money for you." Mary nodded at the women and picked a long piece of pretty white lace from the basket.

"Go to the parlour Charlotte and watch the children for me," and Mary disappeared into the darkness of the cottage behind them. But Charlotte didn't move. Mesmerized again by these women, she just stood gazing at them in silence.

"Let me read your palm Charlotte. Give me your hand." The oldest woman spoke again, bringing her own hand forward towards the girl and Charlotte, as if in a trance, held her upturned hand out for the woman to see.

"What's going on here?" Mary bustled back into the room.
"I can't afford to pay you for a palm reading!"
But as the old gypsy slowly raised her eyes to look straight into Charlotte's; both mother and daughter saw shock and horror on the wizened face.
"This child has my people's blood running through her veins. I see a butcher bringing death into her life. If she stays here with you I see tragedy and a young life cut short before its time."
Turning to Mary the woman reached out to her, "Let us take your daughter now. I see a different path for her if she is living with my people. No tragedy; just a long and happy life."

"You will never take my child. Go away now and don't ever come back. I can look after my own daughter," and Mary, pushing a silver coin into the gypsy's outstretched hand, slammed the door shut in her face and gathered Charlotte into her arms.
"Take no notice of them my love; they are wicked to say such things to you. There is no truth in what she said." But Charlotte was sobbing now, her face buried in her mother's dress.

Suddenly she looked up, "But my father is a butcher, my father is a butcher and he's coming to live with us soon. Mother, I don't want him to come and live with us. Please mother!"

Mary didn't know how to pacify her daughter. She had herself seen what looked like genuine horror in that old woman's face. It had made her blood run cold. Besides this, she had to face the fact again, that Charlotte could be Ben Kircher's child and that the old woman might have seen this connection to her people in the girl's hand. But the rest of it must surely be just a trick to lure her daughter away from her. James would never hurt Charlotte. He loved her. She would never let her go with those travelling people. She didn't belong with them or in their way of life.

Charlotte had never really liked the idea of her father, James Medland, coming to live with them. It had always been just the two of them, Charlotte and her Mother, playing games together, learning things together, singing together as they worked in the cottage. It was the only way of life that she knew and she liked it that way. She'd always been happy when he came around to see them, and he'd made a fuss of her and even given her little presents. But it would be different if he came to live with them. He'd be there every morning when she woke up, every night when she went to sleep.

It wouldn't be her and her mother together anymore; it would be her father and her mother together instead and everything would be different and she would hate it. But she hadn't been afraid before. Now she was afraid.

"Tragedy," the old gypsy woman had said, "a young life cut short." Now she was very afraid and she knew that she had to stop him; stop him from coming to live with them.

"He doesn't care about us," she'd raged at her mother. "If he cared about us he'd have come to live with us a year ago when his wife died."

"Of course he cares for us Charlotte, but he couldn't just come to us, could he? He had his daughters to think about, and what would people have said if he'd just left them and come to live with another woman and her child."

"His other daughters! His daughters! I don't care about his other daughters. I'm supposed to be his daughter aren't I? What about me? He has always put them first. Always."

"Well, he's coming to us now Charlotte. Margaret has married her young man and Elizabeth has gone to live with her aunt in Stratton. But you know all of this. You know that he is selling his house and that he even has plans to sell his business soon. So he won't even be a butcher then, will he? That old gypsy woman has turned your head Charlotte."

"You heard what she said mother. If I stay here with you a butcher will bring death into my life. She saw that in my hand and she was so shocked that she wanted to take me away with her to keep me safe! But if my father stays away from us, I believe that I will be safe with you. Please tell him not to sell his house. He can live up in Poundstock and we can live here, just as it's always been."

But what Charlotte didn't know was that all her pleading and persuading was not going to change her mother's mind. Mary was quite sure that Ben Kircher was behind all of this. She obviously hadn't fooled him that day when they'd met again at Trevalga Inn. He believed that Charlotte was his daughter and somehow he had traced them, and found out what he needed to know about James.   He'd sent those women to their home with a story that would frighten her into letting him take Charlotte away with him. Mary was sure that they would not give up easily.

They would return and maybe he would come with them next time. What if he was so determined to have Charlotte that he would try to steal her away one day? With no one to talk to about all of this, Mary's imagination ran riot. She didn't believe for one moment all that nonsense about a butcher bringing death into Charlotte's life, but she was, nevertheless, very afraid for her daughter's safety. Somehow, she thought, she would have to explain all this to James. Not about Ben of course, but she could tell him about the old gypsy woman's crazy predictions and Charlotte's hysterical reaction. She could even tell him about her own fear that these people would try to take their daughter away from them. James would know what to do. When he came to live with them he would make sure that no harm came to Charlotte. Their dream of being together was so close now that Mary swore to herself that she wasn't going to let anything get in the way of it becoming reality.

The following day was a Sunday and Charlotte should have been getting up early to go to chapel. Instead she lay in her little bed clenching her fists with frustration. Something had come between her and her mother again. The first time had been a year ago when she'd met the gypsy man who'd said that he thought he was her father. He had been sure of it. Her mother had shut her out then and now she was doing it again. The old gypsy woman had been telling the truth. She had been sure of it. What was it about gypsies that seemed to make her mother shut her out, push her away? What if that man really was her father? *"This child has my people's blood running through her veins."* That's what the old lady had said. She'd almost forgotten that. Maybe James Medland wouldn't want to come and live with them if he thought

30

that she wasn't really his daughter, and that her mother had been lying to him all these years.

"When is my father coming to see us next?" Charlotte asked her mother over breakfast that morning.
"Sometime at the weekend I think. Why do you ask child?"
"Because if you won't tell him that you don't want him here anymore, I will have to tell him what that old woman said to us, and he will see why he has to stay away. If he loves us he will stay at Poundstock in his own home."

Mary was shocked. "Charlotte, how can you say these things? She frightened you, I know that. She frightened me as well. But, as time goes by, you will see that it was all nonsense, and when your father is here, he will make sure that no harm comes to you."
"And what if he knew that she'd said I had gypsy blood in my veins. What if he thought that he may not be my father, and that I'd met a gypsy man who is sure that I am his daughter?"

There was no point now in arguing with the girl. She would talk to her when she had calmed down; tell her how much James wanted them to be a proper family, all living together at last. And Charlotte needed to realise that if he left them, they could lose everything, even their home and the little school. Mary was sure that Charlotte would see sense in the end. They had always been so close; mother and daughter, trusting each other, telling each other everything. But she hadn't told Charlotte everything, had she? There were things that you couldn't tell anyone, let alone your own child. Her precious daughter had opened the door to those three gypsy women, and now their whole lives seemed to have turned inside out. Even if Charlotte did see sense, would she be able to live with this fear of James and the death that he was supposed to be bringing to them. Could she ever really trust such a frightened child to keep their secrets? Secrets, which, were they ever to be disclosed, could shatter their lives for ever.

Late that evening, as Mary sat alone, sewing in the fading light, she'd been startled by a gentle tapping on her window. Fearful that her visitor might not be a welcome one, she pulled back the curtain a little and peered out to see who was there. Relieved to see an old and trusted friend outside, she'd realised how much she needed someone to talk to.
"Simon. Come in. It's so good to see you."
"You look worried Mary. Did I give you a shock knocking on the window like that? I know it's late to call, but I've got a message for you from James."
"Well I was alarmed Simon, but I'm happy that you're here. We have a problem and I really don't know what to do about it. I could do with your advice."

Simon Baker kept a beer shop at Trevalga, Churchtown and Mary had known him for as long as she could remember. He was about the same age as James, and the two men were friends, but she'd always seen Simon as more of a father figure; one of those people who seemed to know everything and everyone. He was also a good listener, and ready to help if he could. And so, over a strong brew of tea, Mary told him as much of the story as she had planned to tell James when he came at the weekend; though she was at a loss to know how she could tell him now, with Charlotte's threats hanging over her. At first Simon seemed reluctant to say what he made of it all.

"I've known you for most of your life Mary," he'd said slowly. "and you're a good woman, a good mother. You're not going to like what I have to say to you."

"Go ahead," she'd said. "I know James has always valued your advice. I need, at least, to hear it Simon."

"Well as I see it," he'd said, "there are problems that can only be mended with the passing of time. Charlotte's fears will fade, especially if she doesn't have to face them every day, but your main worry seems to be that these gypsy people may try and snatch her away. I must say I see no sense in it myself, but your fear is real, I can see that. I'm going to suggest that Charlotte goes away for a while; away from James so that she can feel safe, and away from Tresparrett Post so that you can have some peace of mind. I'm sure that one day she will miss you enough to overcome any fears she has left and come home again. James will be here to watch out for her then. These gypsy travellers don't enter the county very often Mary, and when they do, well, news of their whereabouts travels fast. Most times we hear they're at Launceston market before they come this way. We're all on the lookout for them then, aren't we?"

Mary had to agree with him but was badly shaken and had serious doubts. "Where can she go that she would be safe Simon? I don't want her to go very far away. I'll need to know where she is and that she is well and happy."

"Well, as luck would have it Mary, I may have the perfect answer to that problem. I have a little holding close to Bodmin Moor, at a place called Wringfords; only five miles from here as the crow flies. It's just marshland, but I have a few fields and I can sell the sedge for slate packing and make a good profit. These fields all lie near to a sizeable holding, Lower Penhale farm, owned by a widow woman, Phillipa Peter. She's living there with just her son John and a couple of servants. I met John this morning, when I was on my way to my fields, and he happened to say that they are looking for a maid. It seems his brother Edward and his wife were living with them, but his wife's not well and they've gone to live with her mother for a while. They're desperate for a maid Mary; someone to help with the cooking, washing and milking. Charlotte could do that, and she'd be safe out there. The farmhouse is completely surrounded by its own land; no gypsies passing by to take her away. The house is warm, I've been inside and she'd be well fed."

"But Simon, she would be a servant, bound to this Mrs Peter by law, surrounded by strangers. I don't think I can bear that!"

"I could keep an eye on her for you Mary, if that's what's worrying you. Phillipa Peter is well known for her kindness to her servants and John's alright; a bit soft in the head, but he's got a good heart. There are other holdings and tenements all around there, and most of the folk are related, or connected to the Peters in one way or another. I'll even take her out there with me next weekend if you like; see how she gets along. Mrs Peter will be looking to take someone on before the end of the month. It's the end of the spring quarter soon. You'll be able to talk it all over with James then; just the two of you, but I could have a word with him as well if you like. I saw him this afternoon and he asked if I'd let you know that he'd be coming over on Sunday."

"But what if she wants to come home one day Simon and this Mrs Peter won't release her?"

"I know this woman Mary; she's well-liked by everyone; she wouldn't hold anyone against their will. I'm afraid it's the best advice I can give you right now. I'm sure that Charlotte would be safe and happy there for a while."

Phillipa Peter lit a candle on the long table in her farmhouse kitchen. The light was fading as it was near nine-thirty, and with most of the work done, she thought she'd try and read for a while before bedtime. It was hard to concentrate though with the girl wailing and sobbing at the end of the table. Goodness knows she'd tried to pacify her, but all of her efforts had been in vain. Young Will had gone up to bed early just to get away from the noise, and poor John was sitting over on the settle with his hands over his ears. She'd give the girl a day or two but she would have to go back to her mother if she was going to carry on like this. The door opened and Matthew came in, right on time as usual. She expected her servants to be in by nine-thirty as she liked to be settled in bed herself before eleven; they all had an early start in the mornings.

"I'll fix you some supper Matthew," she said and he nodded, sliding into the window seat. It was his way, to sit a while and look out into the gathering darkness, but tonight he seemed more interested in the girl, who was still blubbering and whining; her hands tightly covering her face. He got up to eat his food when she brought it to the table, and sat, a little away from the girl, facing the wall. Picking up her book, Phillipa Peter tried to get back to her reading. There would be little conversation between them with that noise filling her kitchen. But the loud sobbing gradually stopped, turning into little muffled, hiccupping sounds, and looking up, the mistress of the house saw that the child was peeping out between her fingers at an amazing hand shadow of a flying bird on the kitchen wall. The shadow changed into a cat, and then a fox, and the entertainment went on; horses, rabbits, human faces, until the crying finally stopped. And Matthew, without a word, got up from the table, picked up his plate and limped back to the window seat to finish his supper.

Eleven year old Charlotte Dymond watched his movements shyly through swollen, but now dry eyes. She didn't see his lame leg or even the marks on his face left by the smallpox. She only saw a caring, round-faced boy who didn't look much older than herself; the brother she had always longed for.

Early the following evening, Charlotte thought she might explore outside the farmhouse for a while before bedtime. She was feeling a bit better about being sent here now. *"Just for a while my love",* her mother had said, *"just until your father and I have sorted everything out and I am sure that you'll be safe to come home again."* Mrs Peter had been really kind to her all day and not even mentioned her behaviour the night before. There was nothing she could do for now except to make the best of it.

It was a Monday and so, just as it had been at home, she'd worked all day, changing beds, washing sheets and dirty clothes, and then trying to dry them outside, on the hedges around the meadow, at the back and side of the house. She'd already seen all of the inside of the farmhouse. Mrs Peter had helped her strip the beds in the boys' room, as she called it. This was one of the two bedrooms at the front of the house which

John Peter, who had his own bed, shared with Matthew Weeks and another servant, Will Cory. They had to share a bed. Mrs Peter slept in the other bedroom at the front, and a connecting door from her room led into a small middle chamber which was unoccupied. Charlotte had the back bedroom with a window overlooking the meadow. It was much bigger than her room at home and she loved it; except for the dusty curtains. The large kitchen took up most of the area downstairs and there were two doorways, one at the back of the kitchen which led into the meadow, and one at the front, across from the staircase.

Charlotte slipped out of the front doorway, passing through the lean-to porch which led into the front yard. Mrs Peter seemed to be dozing on the settle by the fireplace and probably wouldn't miss her for a few minutes. In the old single-storey buildings across from the house she found the cattle, pigs and a sturdy cart. Looking back across the yard, she saw that the farmhouse wasn't as long as she'd had thought when she first arrived, as it was joined to a large barn with a stable leaning on to its end wall.

Hearing voices and laughter that seemed to be coming from around the side of the house, she set off in that direction and found Matthew and young Will, sitting in the hedge beside a pair of trousers that were still draped over a bit of gorse, drying in the evening sun. Matthew spotted her straight away, "Charlotte. Come and sit with us." He was laughing and biting into an apple.
"We're allowed to eat the windfalls. The mistress doesn't mind. She only picks the best ones for her apple pies."

He waved his arm, pointing at two elderly and scrawny looking apple trees in the corner of the field.

"Here, you can have one," and taking an apple out of his coat pocket he threw it across to her. She caught it and polished it carefully on her skirt, before sitting down beside him and biting into it.

"Mm, it tastes good. Doesn't look like a windfall."

"That's because it isn't" he'd said, and they all three burst out laughing.

Unbeknown to them, Phillipa Peter was outside at the back of the house looking for the missing pair of trousers and she'd seen them laughing together as they sat in the hedge, eating her apples. Smiling to herself she turned and went back inside, leaving them undisturbed. It seemed the girl would fit in after all.

A week flew by faster than any week Charlotte had ever known, and Sunday morning came around again. Mrs Peter was expecting her married daughter Mary to arrive from Halworthy, where she lived with her husband John, and three small children, all under five years of age. John Westlake had called into the farm house on the previous Wednesday to tell his mother-in-law to expect Mary for dinner, but not the children. They would be spending the day with his own mother, Sarah Westlake, who also lived in Halworthy.

"Mother gets lonely, living on her own," he'd said. "She likes to have the children around her for company. And I need to spend some time down on my marsh. So you'll have Mary all to yourself for a while Mother."

Charlotte brought a brew of tea to the table for him and her mistress, and started to pour it out.

"Mary's keen to meet you young Charlotte." His eyes were wandering all over her and then up and down, finally lingering on her face and making her feel uncomfortable.

"We'll look forward to that then won't we Charlotte?" Phillipa Peter broke the sudden unwelcomed silence. "Maybe we can all go to afternoon service together at the chapel."

When Mary arrived, Charlotte took to her straight away. She'd wasted no time in joining them as they peeled the vegetables for dinner and the conversation soon turned to the afternoon service at Tremail Chapel.

"We could all go," Mary had said. "The walk will do us good after one of your Sunday dinners' mother, and I'd like to see the new chapel. I hear the building is almost finished."

Mrs Peter nodded. "There won't be many more services held in the old chapel room, that's for sure."

And so, soon after dinner, Mrs Peter, John Peter, Mary Westlake and Charlotte all left the farmyard by a lane which led to Penhale field, and then crossed Five Acres field to join a track which then took them towards Tremail Chapel. Matthew, it seemed, had been expected to go with them but had, instead, taken himself off for the afternoon to walk on Bodmin Moor and to climb Roughtor.

"They say it's one of the highest hills in Cornwall," he'd said at dinner, whilst tucking into a piece of Mrs Peter's apple pie. "I like to climb to the top and watch the buzzards fly."

Charlotte had thought that it sounded like much more fun than going to chapel, and secretly hoped that one day he would take her out there with him to climb Roughtor and watch the buzzards.

39

The service at Tremail Chapel was held upstairs in an old cottage, in a room accessed by steps, leading up from one side of the building. The room beneath it was being used as horse stables and a caretaker lived in a little two-up-two-down dwelling adjoining the cottage on the other side. Work on the new chapel, which was being built alongside the present one, was well underway and everyone was looking forward to attending services there in the very near future.

It seemed that poor little Charlotte Dymond was the only one there who wasn't happy that afternoon. Feeling shy and awkward amongst so many strangers, she was close to tears and sorely missing her mother. She'd never attended either a church or a chapel without her mother being right there at her side, and now she just felt so small and lonely.

No one appeared to notice the change that had come over her as they walked home together after the short and simple service. John was still singing hymns, quite loudly, while Mrs Peter and her daughter were sharing a long and lively conversation about Mary's three small children, Eliza, Richard and baby Rebecca.

As they drew near to the farm yard at Penhale, Charlotte deliberately slowed her pace and dropped back a little so that the others all reached the house well before her. After watching them go in through the porch, and letting themselves into the kitchen, she slipped away unnoticed and made her way into the barn. It was dark inside, but her eyes soon grew accustomed to the gloom; enough to safely follow the little snuffing and whining noises made by a litter of pups, born in there only three weeks before, and still not venturing very far away from their mother, Issy.

Issy was one of two small terriers that Mrs Peter and John kept on the farm, to catch rats in the barn and around the yard, and keep foxes away from the livestock. It was a job that Issy, a black and white, rough coated young dog, did well; unlike Jack her ginger coated partner in crime and father of her pups. He preferred life outside the farmyard and mostly ran wild in the fields, chasing rabbits and any other small creatures that tried to hide from him in the long grass.

Charlotte had discovered Issy and her pups in the barn three days earlier, and had been sneaking in to see them whenever she could steal a few minutes away from her chores. Issy heard the girl calling to her softly, and just wagged her tail as she lay suckling three pups on their bed of hay. Three more tumbled around her, learning to play-fight together as they waited for their turn to drink their mother's milk. Charlotte sat down beside them, and gathered up the first puppy that approached her, burying her face into the soft, warm, furry little body. Hot tears flowed silently down across her cheeks. Tears of self-pity. Where was her mother? When would she see her again? She was beginning to think that this was all her own fault. Yes, she had been very afraid of the old gypsy woman's warning, but mostly she hadn't wanted to share her mother with the man who, for most of her life, she believed was her father. All her own fault. The puppy began to struggle, trying to release itself from her grasp and so she placed it down carefully, watching it run back to its family. She was feeling very tired now and tomorrow would be a hard day. All that changing beds and washing clothes all over again.
Charlotte thought she would go into the house and just rest for a while on her bed.

As she reached the top of the stairs, she could hear voices coming from Mrs Peter's bedroom.

"My John came home on Wednesday saying he heard old Elias Bettison in the Britannia Beer House calling her the bastard child from Boscastle. Poor friendless little girl, he'd said, born a bastard, just like her mother and her mother's brothers before her." It was Mary's voice, hushed but still clear to Charlotte's young ears.

"Well I won't hear her called that in my house. The poor girl can't help what her mother got up to more than twelve years ago, can she? Or her grandmother either for that matter. Old Elias should be ashamed of himself."

So, her mistress was ready to defend her, even against her own family and neighbours.

"Oh Mother, he meant no harm. He was likely the worse for beer or cider and didn't know what he was saying."

"Well bastard or not her mother's brought her up right. She's worked hard all this week. Saved my poor old bones a lot of work. One morning she was up even before me. I went into her room to wake her and she'd gone. Her bedroom window was open and the curtains missing with her. And when I looked out of the window, there she was, out in the meadow, beating the curtains with a brush. Said they were dusty and didn't think I'd mind if she cleaned them. No Mary, I've only known her a week but I like what I've seen of her. Her mother's done a good job with her and I can't understand why she sent her away. Simon Baker said it was something to do with gypsies trying to take her."

"Well she's a handsome little maid right enough, so maybe they were thinking to steal her away and then sell her on for a pretty penny. Why, even my John said that if she stayed here for a few more blackberry seasons, they'd be calling her *'the belle of Bodmin Moor'* not *'the bastard from Boscastle '*.

Mrs Peter was laughing now. "Well I don't think that will happen somehow Mary. Her mother will want her back before long, you mark my words."

Charlotte crept quietly into her own bedroom and closed the door. It had been just idle gossip between a daughter and her mother. Even at her tender years she knew a little about that. But there was one thing that their conversation had made her sure of. If she ever had children of her own, no-one would be able to call them bastards. She didn't want to be like her mother and her grandmother before that. When she had children, she would be like Mary Westlake, married to their father!

Almost three months passed by before Charlotte got to go out on the moor with Matthew and climb Roughtor. He had other things to do with his evenings and his days off; more interesting things than spending his time around Penhale with a twelve-year old girl. Oh, he liked her well enough; in fact he liked her a lot. She reminded him of his favourite sister, ten-year old Janey. He had three brothers and five sisters and all the girls were younger than him except Mary, who'd married and left home years before, when he was only about the same age as Janey was now.

He was eighteen, not fourteen or fifteen, as Charlotte had thought when their paths crossed on her first night at the farm. The night that she later said she would always remember for the candlelight, and Matthew's magical hand shadows on the whitewashed wall. He'd only been at Penhale himself for three months on that day in June 1838. By sheer coincidence he'd been taken on at Penhale on March 25th, Lady Day, on the recommendation of a member of the same family as Simon Baker, the man who had brought Charlotte to Penhale. His father, John Weeks, had died in 1835 and so his uncle Richard Weeks had taken Matthew on to train as a blacksmith and carpenter in his business at Trekenner in the parish of Lezant, which was close by to Matthew's family home Higher Larrick, also in Lezant and about eleven miles from Lower Penhale Farm in Davidstow parish. Matthew had only been working there for about ten months when misfortune had hit the family once more, and his uncle's wife died.

Heartbroken, Richard Weeks had turned to drink, lost all interest in his business, and sent Matthew to work for John Doney, who was also in the blacksmiths trade in the area around Matthew's home. It had been Mrs Doney, who came from the Baker family in Davidstow, who had heard that Edward Peter and his wife had left Penhale, and that his mother Phillipa Peter had been running the farm for two months with just her 32 year-old son John and a boy servant, Will Cory, who was also her nephew. Will's father, Isaac and another family member Thomas Prout, were coming in to help out whenever they could. Mrs Peter was looking for a live-in male servant and Matthew Weeks, with skills as a carpenter and blacksmith, fitted the bill perfectly.

Besides tending the horses and using his skills making and mending around the farm, Matthew worked on the land with John Peter and young Will. They carried manure to the fields before ploughing for wheat, sowed the seeds, and tended the crop as it grew until it was time for the harvest. The Peters were cattle farmers as well, mostly rearing young bullocks for meat, although Mrs Peter kept a few cows for their milk and made butter and cream just for her own use. There were a handful of pigs in the yard, and chickens to look after as well, so Matthew had more than enough tasks to fill his working day.

In the little time that he had to himself he liked to walk to Halworthy and drink at the local inn. There was a beer house, the Britannia Inn, much closer to Penhale Farm, just over a mile away beside Trevilians Gate on the edge of Bodmin Moor, but Matthew preferred the hustle and bustle of Halworthy Inn, or 'Alldrunkard' as the locals called it. Mainly because of his lame leg, it took him more than an hour to walk to Halworthy, but he was always made welcome by William Northam the landlord and his family. The inn was a hive of activity. Horses fed from their nosebags outside the stables, and local folk conducted their business out in the yard or in the saloon, or played skittles in the alley. Matthew enjoyed just sitting at the bar, listening to stories that people recalled, of the times when the Somerset and Cheshire Militias drank at the inn in the 1790's. Some said that it was from those times that the inn began to be known as 'Alldrunkard'. Others said, jokingly, that it was because the magistrate's sessions were held at the inn, and that the magistrates were all drunkards, rather than all worthy. He'd been told that when prisoners were brought before the magistrate in the parlour, they were handcuffed to a metal bar that reached from floor to ceiling. With the occasional sheep market and the regular dinners that were held there, the place was far more entertaining than the beer house at Trevilians Gate, where the men just gathered to get drunk and talk about gathering sedge from the marshes or cutting peat on the moor.

Sometimes on a Saturday evening Matthew would walk the eleven miles to his family's home at Larrick, near Launceston. He would spend the night and most of the next day there before walking home to Penhale again to start work in the morning. His three brothers, Richard, John and William had themselves all left home, but sisters Hannah, Jane, Elizabeth and Eliza were all still living at home with their mother. It was hardly surprising that, being brought up with so many females around, Matthew Weeks had quite a way with the ladies. It was true that he was lame, with the marks of smallpox on his youthful round face, but winning ways and laughing brown eyes seemed to hold the attention of most of the girls that he met. There was one girl in particular who liked his attention, and it seemed the feeling was mutual. For on his way to or from his home at Larrick Matthew would often linger for an hour or two at the home of 18 year-old Elizabeth Stevens, who lived at Coads Green. They'd been childhood sweethearts since the summer when they'd both helped to bring in the harvest at Matthew's grandfather's farm, and Elizabeth, with her long black hair and rosy red cheeks was still very much his favourite.

July 1838 brought a long dry spell of weather and in early August, at Penhale Farm, the wheat crop was thick on the ground, ears bent over and ready to cut. The day for the start of the harvest was quickly set and the word spread around to their neighbours, who were always more than willing to come along, help bring in the harvest and, at the same time, eat, drink and make merry from morning 'till night. John Peter organised large deliveries of ale and cider, while Mrs Peter and Charlotte spent a whole day baking cakes, buns and puddings. Matthew and Will gathered up rakes and brooms and sharpened up the scythes. They all got up very early in the morning to do the milking and feed the livestock, before the helpers were expected to arrive, all meeting up in the wheat field for their breakfast before starting the work of the day. It would be hard, backbreaking labour but the promise of good food, good ale and when the work was done, a good time at the harvest supper, never failed to bring the helpers to the farm.

Only twelve months before, Charlotte had followed the scythe, gathering up swaths of wheat and tying them up in bands, over at Dunes farm near her own home at Tresparrett Post. The farmer's daughters, Honor and Evelyn, had been coming to her mother's school for several months, and they asked if she would like to help bring in the harvest. She'd spent quite a lot of time out on their farm after that, learning to milk the cows and to ride her friends' ponies. It had stood her in good stead for when she had suddenly found herself living at Lower Penhale. But this year, Charlotte would not be following the scythe in the fields, for the workers had to be fed and watered. With the remains of breakfast all cleared away, work began preparing their dinner. Only the best meat and vegetables were to be used. Mary Westlake had come over to help cook, and then carry the meals into the field. Dinner was served between midday and one o'clock, along with more helpings of ale and cider, which had already been distributed generously throughout the morning. The liquor it seemed had raised everyone's spirits, and Charlotte could hear the noise of their joking and laughter from quite far away, as she helped to bring them their meals from the farmhouse.

She was on what she hoped was her last trip to and from the field when she saw Will Cory and Matthew sitting under an old oak tree near the gate; both with empty tankards in their hands, and their eyes closed as they rested for a short while before two o'clock, when all the work would start again.

"I trust you two have had your dinners," she called across to them, and Matthew, opening one eye, smiled and patted the ground beside him.

"We're full and fit to bust," he'd said, "Sit down with us. I'm sure you deserve to be still for a while."

He tipped his hat over his eyes, trying to shut out the sun, and lapsed once more into silence. Charlotte, glad to steal a few minutes away from work, sat down beside them under the tree, and hearing some tuneless singing break out across the way, began to hum the music from 'London's Burning' quietly to herself.

Matthew, pushing his hat back, sat up and started grinning at her.

"Why are you always singing that? If it's not that, it's silly nursery rhymes. 'Hush-a-bye Baby', or 'Hickory Dickory Dock'!"

"Or 'Oranges and Lemons'," Will joined in, chuckling to himself.

"Well, we used to sing them at home all the time. We taught them to the children who came to my mother's school." Charlotte began to scramble to her feet, looking upset.

"Well we'll have to teach you some new songs then won't we? Songs you can sing at the harvest supper," and catching her by the arm Matthew pulled her down to sit beside him again.

"I know the 'The Faithful Plough'," she said, still sounding wounded, "and some others, I'm sure!"

"Well that's a start then. But I'll wager you don't know this one; and he broke into song, quickly joined by Will.

"Adam and Eve would never believe
That Peter the miller was dead,
Shut up in the tower for stealing of flour
And forced to lose his head."

Charlotte though, was not to be won over by their merriment.

"Well I'm not singing that one," she said, "forced to lose his head indeed! I don't like it." She hugged her knees, shaking a little.

"Well it's no worse than your 'Oranges and Lemons'. That has, 'Here comes a chopper to chop off your head'!" Will was shaking with laughter now. Well fuelled by cider, he was finding all this quite hilarious.

"What's wrong with you two, shivering on such a hot day? Are you sickening for something?" Tom Prout was standing in front of them, greedily supping his ale.

"No," replied Will, "we've just spooked Charlotte with one of the harvest songs."

Tom went on his way, shaking his own head in disbelief.

But Charlotte was still hugging her knees and shuddering, "Here comes a chopper to chop off your head," she muttered, as if she'd only just heard the words for the first time. Matthew began to feel sorry for her. The songs that she sang probably just reminded her of happier days, and he began to feel bad now for laughing at her. "You know Charlotte," he said, "I was thinking earlier that when the harvesting is all over, I'd like to go out and climb Roughtor again. And I was wondering if you would like to come out there with me. The girl's beaming smile was reward enough for sacrificing his planned day of solitude. And 'Peter the Miller' was quite forgotten.

With the beguiling promise of a walk on Bodmin Moor to watch the buzzards fly, the remaining days of the harvest seemed far too many for little Charlotte Dymond. The days seemed endless, for at five o'clock when the afternoon work was done, more liquor was carried out to the fields, along with panniers of buns and cakes, and when, and only when, all this had been consumed, work commenced again until the end of the day. The helpers then all converged on the farm house to drink some more, and talk and sing until the early hours of the morning.

Charlotte was exhausted, and groaned in silent despair when she realised that it was not only the wheat at Lower Penhale that had to be reaped, but also the crop at Rosebenault, whose neighbouring fields, tenanted by the Prout family, were also owned by Mrs Peter and her son John. Finally the last load was ready to be brought in from the field, escorted by all the helpers. The last sheaf was gathered, and one of the workers lifted it up above his shoulder.
"We have it!" he shouted, and the reply came back to him "What 'ave 'ee?"
"A neck!" called the worker and everyone cheered.
This last sheaf was plaited and brought in with the load, carried beside the cart. It was then given to Mrs Peter in the farmhouse kitchen, where it would stay according to custom, until the next harvest.

And then it was time for the games, to be followed in the evening by a big harvest supper with pork and potatoes, cheese and apple dumplings, cakes, plum pudding and cream. Charlotte wondered where they got their energy from, all scrambling about for apples and then for hot pennies. And then came the feasting, held in the barn, to be followed by singing and dancing.

Mrs Peter, it seemed, was more than a little affected by the occasion, and was shedding tears into her pocket handkerchief for 'her poor dead husband Richard'.

"He would have loved to have seen us like this," she wept, "all together and with the harvest safely brought in."

"Oh, I'm sure that he's still watching over you." said Charlotte, trying to comfort her. I should think that he's been watching you all through the days of the harvest."

"Oh I do hope so, Charlotte, I really do. And his dear sister, over there with her family, she would be happy to hear your words, for she was very fond of her brother. I shall tell her straight away," and still dabbing her eyes with her handkerchief, she moved away towards the Prout family, who occupied the cottage on her adjoining holding at Rosebenault.

Charlotte looked around for someone else to talk to, but she didn't know many of the people who were gathered there together in the barn; most of them now in very high spirits. Mary Westlake was talking and laughing with the old man who'd helped John Peter unload all the beer and cider for the harvest. He was Humphrey Vosper, the owner of the Britannia beer house over six fields away, on the edge of Bodmin

Moor, a close neighbour of young Will's parents Isaac and Maria Cory and of Sampson Prout at Moorshead.

Will was sitting across the room on a hay bale beside Matthew, so Charlotte made her way over to them.
"I didn't know that the Prout brothers were the mistress's nephews," she said, sitting down beside them.
"Every last one of them, Samson, Thomas and John. Everyone's related 'round 'ere Charlotte, 'cept for you and me."
Matthew's words were slurred and he turned to Will, slapping him on the shoulder. "Why even young Will here's related to the mistress."
"Is that true Will?" Charlotte asked as Will got up, glaring at Matthew and rubbing his shoulder.
"Well I know Tom Prout's my cousin, so I s'pose he's right," and giving Matthew a playful, but well aimed kick on the shin, he shuffled off towards his parents on the other side of the barn.

Someone close by was playing the fiddle and the dancing had started but Charlotte was feeling sleepy now. The last few days had been very tiring and the inside of the barn was so hot. She looked around for her mistress or Mary Westlake but her eyes lit on someone who seemed to be watching her intently.
"Who is that man over there Matthew? You know everybody. He keeps looking over at us."
But Matthew couldn't recall seeing the man anywhere before.
"Aven't a clue Charlotte, probably someone the master hired in Bodmin to help with the harvest. Anyone who helps can come to the supper. He looks like a traveller to me."

"I'm sure I've seen him somewhere," said Charlotte sleepily, her head dropping onto Matthews shoulder. As she fell into an exhausted sleep, Matthew grimaced at the smiling stranger. So much for his hopes of a dance and a stolen kiss or two with one of the pretty young servant girls. Oh well, Charlotte wasn't the only one who was tired, and his ankle had been hurting quite badly this last day or so. And so he resigned himself to just sitting there, enjoying his ale, and very soon he was dozing beside her. Mrs Peter noticed them and smiled to herself for she thought, they always seemed so content in each other's company.

Matthew couldn't quite understand the change that had come over Charlotte that morning. She had been looking forward to their day out on Bodmin Moor, and had seemed so excited as they'd walked through the fields, crossed the strip of common land, and the road between Camelford and Altarnun. She'd skipped past the Britannia Inn at Trevillian's Gate; Sampson Prout's home at Moorshead, and even run ahead of him as they started to make their way across the moor towards the boggy ground beneath Lanlary Rock, the white stoned landmark that he'd told her about that morning before they'd left the farmhouse. At first he'd wondered if he'd be able to keep up with her, but then she'd suddenly turned back and returned to walk beside him, trudging along with her head down.

"What's the matter Charlotte? Tired already? We've got at least two more miles to walk before we get to the top of Roughtor."

At first she didn't answer him. She didn't want to answer him. He'd been kind to her, bringing her out

53

here with him on the one day of the week that he didn't have to work, and now, all she wanted to do was to turn around and go back to the farm. There was a strange heaviness inside her, weighing her down, making her ill at ease and unhappy.

"It's lonely out here Matthew," was all that she was able to say.

"How can it be lonely? I'm here with you aren't I?"

"But there are no other people. Just sheep and wild looking horses with tangled manes. And there are no cottages, or barns, just grass and stones and hills." She stopped walking and stood looking across towards Roughtor, feeling guilty now because she didn't want to spoil Matthew's day. It hadn't been easy for him to get permission for her to go walking on the moor with him on his first free Sunday after the harvest. Mrs Peter had, at first, been set against their plan to climb Roughtor together.

"I'm not sure that I like this idea Matthew," she'd said, looking quite shocked when they'd first mentioned it to her.

"It can be dangerous out there, and how do I know you'll look after her?"

"I'll take care of her mistress," he'd said. "She'll be safe with me. I'm use to looking after my little sisters, and taking them out when I go back home. And well, I have promised Charlotte now that I'll take her along."

"Well you had no right to promise her. I don't know what her mother would think of me, letting you take her off like this on your own, or Simon Baker for that matter if he found out."

"How's he going to find out mistress, if we don't tell him? And as for her mother, well it don't seem like she's very bothered. She hasn't been out here to see her, or had her back home has she? Not once since she sent her out here with Simon Baker. She didn't even come out here with them to settle her in."

Charlotte had found herself quite startled by Matthew's words. She hadn't realised how strongly he felt about her mother.
But at first it had seemed that their mistress' mind would not be altered.
"I really don't like this Charlotte," she'd said, "I really don't like this at all."
And she'd gone back to her work, sewing a button on to John Peter's shirt, and not mentioned the matter again for the rest of the day.
It had been early the following morning, as Charlotte came down over the stairs to help with the milking that she had heard Mrs Peter and John talking together in the kitchen.
"I feel really sad for that girl John," her mistress was saying. "Shut away here on the farm. I'm not used to having such a young maid here with no family to turn to. Matthew's right about her mother. I'm thinking that I might take Charlotte to market in Bodmin with me next time I go, and if her mother finds out and doesn't agree, then she'll just have to fetch her back home again, won't she?"
"You fuss too much mother," John had said, "Let them go spend a day out watching buzzards if that's what they want."

Matthew had, by then, joined her on the stairs, and overhearing John's words he'd grinned and gone down past her, into the kitchen on his own.
"Ah Matthew," she heard her mistress say, "I've been talking to John and we've decided that Charlotte can go along with you on Sunday to Roughtor. I don't suppose you'll let her come to any harm. But only this

once now. Don't want you going out there together every Sunday. Charlotte should be coming to chapel with me. And what I'm supposed to say to the folk who ask after her out there at Tremail, I really don't know."

Later in the week, as they'd worked together around the house, her mistress had spoken, quite wistfully Charlotte thought, of days when she herself had walked on the moor with her husband Richard and their children.

"We used to climb up Roughtor," she'd said, *"and walk along the top of it to Showery Tor. We even climbed Brown Willy once, but it's higher than Roughtor and at least a mile further on towards Blisland, so I never went that far out again. Fair killed me it did! One day we walked out to see if we could find the old tinners' shelter next to Roughtor Ford stream works. It's still out there Charlotte."*

And she'd gone on to tell her everything she knew about the days when Bodmin Moor had been an important area where tin could be found and mined. She'd spoken of times hundreds of years before when people lived right out on the moor, settling together in little hamlets, farming the land and grazing their animals, much as they did today at Lower Penhale.

"Do you want to turn back Charlotte?" Matthew had been watching her as she stared up at Roughtor, lost in her own thoughts. "I can come out here again later, or another day. I don't mind."

"No Matthew, we'll walk on," she answered him quietly. "The mistress might never let me out of her sight again if she thought I was frightened of a bit of grass and a few stones."

Now it was his turn to reward her with a beaming smile.

"Brave girl," he said. "Here you can carry this for a while," and he handed her the small basket that he'd been holding, packed up with pasties and apples for their dinner.

There was a wry smile on his face as he said "You count the horses. I'll count the sheep. And the one who counts the most gets the biggest pasty!" He liked pasties!

The heaviness that Charlotte had felt inside her had all but gone when she'd reached the top of the tor and fallen to her knees, too worn out to even look around at the views. Matthew was close behind her, and reaching the top, he sat down straight away and began to unpack the food.

Tucking into that pasty dispersed the last little bit of weight in Charlotte's chest, and as she gazed quietly around and across at Brown Willy, her spirits began to soar again with the birds that flew above them. For a while they sat in silence, just watching for buzzards and looking down at the sheep and horses below, now just tiny specks on the landscape.

"What's that down there," Charlotte had asked, pointing at some land around Brown Willy. "It looks as if someone's marked out the ground into strips."

"They're the old strip fields," Matthew told her. "It's the way they used to farm years ago. Some of those strips would be prepared for crops and some would be sown with grass. The thick turf that grew would be skimmed off and burnt when it was dry. The ashes would go back into the land."

"How do you know all this Matthew?" Charlotte had asked him. "I thought you were a blacksmith by trade and had only just come into farming."

"My grandfather was a farmer," he replied, "not far from here at Trecrogo in South Petherwin. He died only last year. My father was his eldest son, but he passed away three years ago, and my uncle Richard took over his estate. Farmers are always talking of the old times Charlotte, and the old ways of farming the land haven't changed too much around here."

"So if your father was still alive, you could be working on your own family's land now, instead of here at Penhale?"

Matthew nodded and handed her an apple.

"But I count myself lucky to have such a kind mistress Charlotte. And so should you. There's not many that would have packed us up with this food today, when it was our choosing not to be back in time for dinner."

"Well I made the pasties myself, and picked the apples, and packed it all up in the basket. So it's really my doing that we have dinner today."

"No Charlotte," and Matthew shook his head, laughing. He was teasing her now. "The mistress gave you the beef and vegetables for those pasties, out of the kindness of her heart, so I say, it was her doing!"

But his attempt at humour was lost on her because, it seemed, she had stopped listening to him.

"How did you come by your lame leg?" she asked him, frowning and looking at his boots. "The toe turns up on your right boot, and not on your left!"

Matthew shook his head again, this time in disbelief, for this was how Charlotte reminded him of his sister

Janey, asking questions of people that no-one else would venture to ask.

"It was after I'd recovered from the smallpox," he said. "I was only seven years old and my leg was like everyone else's before that. I got better, but my ankle hurt me so much that I was forced to limp as I walked, and as I grew my ankle wouldn't move as it should, and grew misshapen. My mother still blames the smallpox for my lame leg." He stood up, brushing pastry crumbs down onto the ancient stones around his feet.

"Come on young lady; let's get you back before the mistress sends out a search party for us."

It was on the last few feet of their descent from *'Matthews Mountain',* as Charlotte was calling it now, that she looked up when a bird called out above them, and lost her footing on some loose stones. She slid, just a little way, but then, unable to save herself, she fell backwards, her left leg buckling underneath her as she screamed out in pain.

"I can't move," she cried, "Matthew I can't move my leg. I think I've broken it!"

"Stay still!" he ordered her, "we'll have to get you back to the farm somehow, but we'll have to rest here for a while and see if it gets any easier."

Her face was white and distorted with pain, but gradually, as time passed, she was able to move her leg into a more normal position and thought that she might, with Matthew's help, be able to struggle to her feet. She was still in a lot of discomfort, but they had to get off the moor, and so, together, they limped along, only stopping to rest when the pain grew so intense that she could go no further. They'd reached Lanlary rock when Matthew wondered if he should go on alone to Isaac Cory's house, or to the Britannia Inn where they could make up some sort of stretcher to carry her back to the farmhouse. But Charlotte's face grew even paler at his suggestion.

"Matthew," she said sounding horrified, "you can't leave me out here on my own. I couldn't bear it. Please don't ever leave me out here on the moor alone!" And so Matthew lifted her up onto his back and with her arms wrapped so tightly around his neck that at times she was almost strangling him, they eventually made their way right back to the farmhouse on their own, for they found there was no one at home at either the inn, or at Isaac Cory's house.

"Lord save us!" exclaimed Mrs Peter as they burst through her kitchen door, and Matthew staggered across the slate floor to lay Charlotte down on the settle. "What have you done to the girl Matthew?"

"I haven't hurt her mistress." Matthew protested and Charlotte quickly spoke up for him.

"Don't blame him mistress. It was all my fault. I slipped and fell at the foot of Roughtor and I think I've broken my leg. Matthew's had to carry me near half the way back."

"We need to thank the lord then," said John Peter, who'd left his seat at the table and come across to see what was going on, "For if you'd slipped at the top of Roughtor, Matthew could never have brought you back here on his own."

Fortunately for everyone at Penhale, Charlotte hadn't broken her leg, but it was badly twisted at the knee and very swollen.

Much later that evening, with Charlotte tucked up safely in her bed, Mrs Peter came to sit at the kitchen table with her son and Matthew.

"You see what I mean now," she'd grumbled, looking across at her son. "This is when that girl should go home to her mother for a while, and I could get someone in to help me with the work. But there'll be no chance of that, you mark my words."

"Mother." said John, trying to stay patient "Charlotte's young, she'll mend soon enough and we'll be alright. We managed for a few months before she came here and we'll manage again. Matthew will do the milking for you and Mary will come over to help. She's always glad of an excuse to leave the children with Sarah Westlake, and spend time with us, even if she does have to work while she's here."

John Peter, thought Matthew, sometimes, even if it wasn't very often, spoke a lot of sense.

February 1839

The carpentry skills that Matthew had learnt in the ten months he'd spent with his uncle at Trekenner in Lezant were proving to be invaluable to the Peter family. He had brought the tools that he owned with him and, whenever the barn roof needed repairing, the old cart had to be fixed, a milking stool or chopping board needed replacing, Matthew was on hand to do the job. As well as this, his training in the blacksmith trade, with both his uncle and John Doney, was more than useful to John Peter; It was saving him a lot of money. It was February now, a quiet time on the farm, and the stable badly needed a new floor. It was almost dangerous in places and they'd been planning the work for months. Finally, all the preparations had been made and Matthew had gone off after breakfast to make a start on the job, so John Peter was surprised to see him coming back into the kitchen half an hour later, looking red in the face and quite angry.

"I've been looking for my hammers," he said, "I had two in the old shed but I can't see them anywhere. And now Will's saying that he saw Tom Prout with them yesterday."

Phillipa Peter nodded. "That's right. He took them to mend the door to the piggery. I saw him working on it."
"So what's he done with them then? I can't start the work without them. He's always using my things and not putting them back. I swear he does it to annoy me."
"Well he's done that alright then hasn't he?" said John, laughing and slapping the table.

"Matthew, we all know that you and Tom have got no time for each other, but I'm sure that he doesn't go out of his way just to annoy you." His mistress spoke firmly. "Now if you look in the piggery, I'm sure you'll find your hammers."

But, instead of going back outside to start his search again, Matthew sat down at the table with a new, and determined look in his eyes. "We've never got on," he said, "We worked together years back, on a farm in Lezant, lived in the same house for a while …………"

Mrs Peter interrupted him. "Well you don't have to live with him now do you? He doesn't even work here. But he is my nephew Matthew, and he likes helping out at Penhale, has done since he was a boy. And I like having him around, so I'm afraid you'll just have to make the best of it."

Matthew looked down at the table. He had something to say and this seemed like a good time to say it.
"I thought," he said, looking back up at John Peter. "I thought master, that I might fix up the old shed. It needs some work doing on it anyway and it's big enough for me to have a workshop there, for the carpentry. I can make a bigger workbench and a tool box for the hammers and chisels and saws. We could turn it into two sheds, one for the cart and the farm tools and one for the workshop. Different doors. And I could lock up my side of it."

John Peter was laughing again. "Do what you like Matthew," he said, "it's alright with me. But no locks eh Mother? We don't lock the doors on the house, so I don't think we're going to start locking up the sheds."

"And I'll have a word with my nephew. Ask him to put your tools back where he finds them next time. Now I must make a start on the vegetables or there'll be nothing for us to eat at dinner time."

"I'll look in the piggery then," said Matthew looking happier now and jumping up from the table, "And when I finish the stable floor, I'll make a start on the shed. It'll take a month or so, but it'll fill up my time until the farm work really starts up again."

He was still muttering quietly as he let himself out through the kitchen door. "And, if I can't lock the shed, I might just put a lock on my tool box."

May, 1839 – Bodmin Market

It was a Saturday morning and Phillipa Peter was going into Bodmin Market with her son John, as soon as her morning chores were done. She was looking forward to it, as she hadn't been away from the farm for weeks, except to go to chapel at Tremail most Sundays, and just that once to Davidstow Church, for their special service at Easter. She looked across the kitchen at Charlotte, who was busy as usual, and singing away to herself quietly as she cleared away the last of the breakfast dishes. That poor girl never goes anywhere she thought. It's a crying shame. And she remembered how she'd vowed to herself to take Charlotte to market with her one day. But that had been before the girl's accident out on the moor, when she'd so badly hurt her leg. It had taken weeks to mend, that leg, much longer than any of them had expected, but Charlotte hadn't complained once, carrying on with whatever little jobs she could manage around the farm. She'd peeled all the vegetables, mended and ironed the men's shirts; even helped with the milking, with her little leg stuck out straight in front her, because she couldn't bend it. And all with a smile on her pretty little face. Since then they'd harvested the corn in late September, threshed the crops in early winter, celebrated Christmas all together and she still hadn't taken the poor child to market.

"How would you like to come into Bodmin with the master and me this morning Charlotte?" she asked. And her little maid was so shocked that she dropped the plate she was holding straight down onto the hard slate floor, where it smashed into dozens of little pieces.

65

"Oh mistress? I'm so sorry". She bent down to start to pick them up, but her mistress stopped her.

"Don't worry about that Charlotte. It was only an old plate. I'll clear it all up. You get away upstairs and wash your face. You're coming with me. Oh, and put on your Sunday dress child. I want Bodmin to see my pretty little maid at her best.

It was all of twelve miles from Lower Penhale farm, across moorland and countryside into Bodmin town. On the final part of their journey, a fairly arduous descent, on a narrow track, John Peter started to whistle a little tune.

"We're 'ere now Charlotte," he called back to her cheerfully.

"It's John's favourite market," Mrs Peter said to her, "but it's too far for me to travel more than two or three times a year."

They were nearing the bottom of the hill before Charlotte saw the four spires of a large church tower; and then the church itself, standing tall beside it's town, splendid in the morning sunlight.

"They must be very proud, the people who live here," Charlotte said, turning around in her seat to get a view of the front of the church as they passed it by, and made towards the town, "it's beautiful!"

"It's hundreds of years old, or so I've been told," said her mistress. "But turn back around here now child; look at all these market stalls!"

John Peter drove their horse and cart up through the street, making his way to the Royal Hotel where he planned to stable the horse for a few hours, and Charlotte was surprised to find that so many people called out to greet Mrs Peter and her son and amiably stood aside to let them pass by.

"Everyone seems to know you mistress?" she said, smiling up at the woman she was growing so fond of. They were standing together outside of the Royal Hotel, having left John inside to 'have a drink or two' before going about his own business.

Mrs Peter patted Charlotte on the arm.

"Well we've lived around these parts a good number of years, so I'd expect them to know us by now. Follow me Charlotte and I'll introduce you to some of our friends." And she set off back down the street so quickly that Charlotte found herself struggling to keep up. As dodging the horse dung was proving to be impossible, she hoisted her skirts up around her ankles and jostled her way through the smelly, crowded street, while keeping her eyes firmly fixed on Mrs Peter's grey bonnet. As she came to an area where the street divided up into three different directions, she could see her mistress standing over to her right, at the foot of some steps which led up towards a very large and grand looking building which Charlotte knew was the new purpose built courthouse, only finished and opened the summer before, just after she had been sent to live at Lower Penhale. Mrs Peter was talking to a young fair haired lady who turned and smiled at Charlotte as she walked up to them.

"Ah, here she is Tamson. This is my little maid. Charlotte, this is Mrs Chapman. You know John Chapman the butcher? Well this is his wife." And Charlotte found herself looking into bright, friendly blue eyes that straight away dispersed the shyness that she so often suffered when meeting people for the first time.

"I hear you're almost thirteen now Charlotte," Mrs Chapman was saying, "That's the same age as my little sister. I miss her sorely now that I'm married and living apart from her. You must come and visit with me sometimes on your day off. I'll be glad to have your company. We live at Trevivian. It's only a short distance from Lower Penhale. Do you know the house?"

Charlotte did, as she walked right past it whenever she attended Tremail Chapel, but it was Mrs Peter who broke in and answered for her.

"That's just what Charlotte needs as well Tamson; some young female company. It'll be good for her to get away from the farm sometimes. Maybe she could call in on you next Sunday after chapel."

With the visit to Trevivian all arranged they parted company with Tamson Chapman, but Charlotte was full of questions about her as she trotted along beside her mistress, determined this time to keep up with her.

"Why have I never seen Mrs Chapman before? Don't they ever go to the chapel? How old do you think she is mistress? She looks very young."

"I declare I haven't seen you so excited since you went out to Roughtor with Matthew!" Phillipa Peter was delighted to see that Charlotte seemed happy about the arrangement they'd made.

"Well, John Chapman has never been one to attend chapel. He's a staunch churchgoer that one. Goes to Davidstow Church every Sunday and I expect young Tamson goes with him now that they're married. John only married her a few weeks back. She's from Week St Mary, not far away, but I have no idea how old she is Charlotte. Not many years older than you I should think. Now we must call in at the draper's and you can meet an old friend of mine, Mrs Helson. I'm hoping she'll have some material that we can use to make new drapes for your bedroom window. I noticed those old ones looked quite threadbare when we washed them last week. Here we are now. You'll like Mrs Helson Charlotte, I'm sure."

Charlotte did like Mrs Helson. She was small and round with twinkly eyes and face that smiled even when she wasn't smiling.
"I've heard all about you from Phillipa," she said, fussing around Charlotte like a mother hen. "We weren't blessed with daughters Charlotte, but we have two strapping sons and if we ever have granddaughters, well I hope they'll be as pretty as you are."
Charlotte wasn't sure what she was supposed to say after that, so as the two older women began to chatter and laugh together, and seek out suitable material for window drapes, she turned and focused her attention on the people passing by the door and window in the street outside. The light was very dim inside the shop and the air smelt and even tasted slightly musty. Just as she began to hope that Mrs Peter wouldn't spend too long talking with her old friend, the shop door opened and a woman stood, framed in the entrance, peering in as if waiting for her eyes to adjust to the dark interior.

Another customer; this would hurry things along a little, but then, as recognition dawned, Charlotte gasped and Mrs Peter turned to see who was causing the problem. Together they watched as a man appeared behind the woman and slid one arm around her waist, holding her tightly to him. Almost at the same time his other arm appeared at her throat, holding a large butchers knife that glinted, even in the weak sunlight, as he turned the sharp edge towards her. It was Mrs Peter's turn to gasp, but as she watched, the woman reached up and gently pulled the blade away from her throat. Laughing, she turned to face the man and taking the knife from him, she twisted it and ran her finger along the top edge of the blade, as if she was admiring it. Taking it from her he pointed towards the shop doorway, as if asking whether or not she wanted to go inside, but she shook her head and linked her arm through his as they turned and walked away together.

"He was just fooling around, that's all. That was probably a new knife that he's bought in the market and he was just showing it off to his lady friend." It seemed that Mrs Helson had also been watching the little scene in the street outside, and was now trying to turn her customer's attention back to the material that she was buying, but Mrs Peter could see tears welling up in Charlotte's eyes.
"What's the matter child? Do you know that woman?"
"She's my mother, mistress. And that man, well he's the man who thinks he is my father."
Her bitter words were softly spoken, but the impact silenced the older women for several moments.
"Well I think we'll buy that material Charlotte and when we've done all the shopping, we'll go home and sort this out. There's more to your story then you've told me, and indeed, more than Simon Baker ever told me. I think it's time I knew the truth."

That evening after supper, under the pretence of measuring up the new material for window drapes,

Mrs Peter left John and Matthew to their own devices in the kitchen and followed Charlotte upstairs to the her bedroom.

"The drapes will wait," she said, shutting the door firmly behind her. "I want to know why your mother sent you away from your home Charlotte. Simon Baker told me that she was living in fear of your being snatched away by some gypsy women who seemed to believe that you had gypsy blood in you and that, if you stayed with your mother, a butcher would bring death to your door. I have heard from Elias Bettison that a butcher by the name of Medland is your father; James Medland he called him, but that you had never lived together as a family. Simon led me to believe, that, as time passed by, your mother would realise that this old gypsy's curse was all nonsense, and that she would want you to come home again. He said your father would be living there with your mother quite soon, and that he would sort everything out and make sure that you would be safe. Am I right Charlotte? You led me to believe earlier today that Mr Medland may not be your father. Is this true?"

Slowly and reluctantly, Charlotte began to tell the story, as she knew it, of the life that she had lived before being brought to Lower Penhale Farm by Simon Baker. And as Mrs Peter tried to unravel the tangled tale of lies and love which seemed to end with a gypsy's curse, she still couldn't understand why the girl's mother seemed to have completely abandoned her.

"But why has she not asked to see you? Almost a year has passed now and you haven't seen her at all until today. Simon Baker said that you and your mother had seemed inseparable and that your father had always provided for you both. I understand that he is quite well-to-do. If you were to go back to live with them, I'm sure that you would never have to go into service again. Are you still afraid of that old gypsy woman's words Charlotte? Are you afraid of your father?"

"He is not my father mistress. I believe that the travelling man I met at Trevalga Inn is my real father. And I can see now that it was my fault that my mother sent me away; my fault that she doesn't want me back. I told her that if Mr Medland ever came to live with us, I would tell him the truth; tell him that he wasn't my father. I didn't want him with us mistress; I couldn't bear to think about it. We were happy without him and I just wanted him to stay in his house in Poundstock and leave us to live together at Tresparrett Post. I didn't want anything to change. I didn't want to share her with him!"

"And did you feel that way before the old gypsy woman told you that a butcher would bring tragedy into your life?"

"Yes mistress. My mother always said that one day he would come to live with us and we would be a proper family. But I didn't want that to ever happen to us. I wanted him to stay with his other family. I used to pray that his wife wouldn't die, and that he would have to stay there for years and years to look after her."

"But Charlotte, didn't you think about what might have happened to you and your mother if you had told him about this gypsy man who said that he was your father? He might have thrown you out of your home. You could have lost everything. Your mother may have had to go into service, or into the workhouse with you. I can see now how all this came about, but I don't know what we can do about it. Have you changed Charlotte? Could you go back to them now and live with them as a family; say nothing of this other man. Could you do that?

"No mistress, I don't believe that I could. I am afraid of what I might do if I had to share my mother with him."
"So you would rather lose her altogether would you? Never see her again? Really Charlotte, I don't understand you at all, but you can stay here as long as needs be and maybe all of this will work itself out one day, for I'm sure there's nothing I can do about it. Good night child. I'll see you in the morning and we'll say nothing of this to the men folk. Best kept between ourselves Charlotte, for I don't know what would happen to your mother if Mr Medland got to hear of it."

Phillipa Peter didn't sleep easy that night. Her little maid had a side to her that she didn't like or understand. She'd have to keep an eye on her, for it seemed that the girl was her own worst enemy. God help any man who one day got too close to Charlotte Dymond. His life wouldn't be easy. That much she was sure of.

December 1839

The arrival of eighteen year old Rebecca Jewell in the close knit community surrounding Penhale farm caused something of a stir. A farm servant girl, employed by the Hockens of Trevivian, close neighbours to John and Tamson Chapman, she was also closely related to Mrs Peter's family and so, well connected, if not well-to-do.

Henry and May Hocken had fields which adjoined the Peter's land, as well as some of John Chapman's land, and as neither of them were in good health in the autumn of 1839, extra help was needed on the farm and Rebecca Jewell came well recommended.

"She's a sweet girl, but they say she's quiet, very shy," Phillipa Peter told her nephew Tom Prout when he asked her about Rebecca one morning in the yard. "I'd like to get to know her better," he'd said, "but I thought she might be a bit fiery, with that red hair!"
"Oh I don't think so Tom, and if you're interested, I think you'll have to do the chasing. She's not the type of girl to come around here looking for you!"

There were times when she despaired for Thomas. He was, although she would never admit it, her favourite nephew. All three brothers were fine young men in her eyes, but Tom had so many ways about him that reminded her of her dear husband. As a small child, the eldest of the three boys, Sampson, hadn't been able to pronounce her name and had called her 'Aunt Pippy'. Thomas and John had naturally followed him. She'd always been 'Aunt Pippy' to them. But now that they were all grown men, it was 'Aunt Phillipa'; though she guessed that when

74

they were talking amongst themselves she was still 'Pippy' to her nephews. Sam had long since settled down with a wife and family. She rarely saw him these days. John, the youngest, was always fooling about, but he was sensible, worked hard and looked after his money. Tom mostly lived at home, at Rosebenault, but it felt to her as if he was just floating, not wanting to put down roots. He helped at home, hired himself out and worked for anyone who had need of him, and turned up at Penhale to work just for the love of it. As far as she knew he drank all of his money away, and put very little effort into courting any of the young girls who took his fancy. One day she supposed he'd find his way and be happy, for that was the thing that worried her most. Was he happy?

It was early December when Matthew noticed Rebecca Jewell, leaving Penhale farmhouse, carrying a little basket as usual and fastening her bonnet against the cold. He was leading John Peter's horse out of the stable. His master had asked him over breakfast if he would check the horse over that morning, as he'd thought him a mite lame when he'd ridden him back from Halworthy late the night before. Tom Prout came out of the old shed with a food bucket, and stopped briefly, looking over at Rebecca before disappearing into the piggery. Rebecca's visits to Mrs Peter were quite frequent but as she normally hurried off without even a glance in his direction, Matthew was surprised when she turned, apparently noticing the horse, and walked quickly towards him. The horse was part shire, black as midnight with a white blaze on his face and white feathered feet. He always attracted attention.

"Such a handsome animal," she said, "is he kept just for riding?"

"He's the master's horse, but he does draw the cart and the plough when he's needed."

"What do you call him?" asked Rebecca, obviously fascinated, but standing back a little nervously.

"The master named him Hercules. He's strong but he won't hurt you. You can stand closer."

She held up her hand. "No, no, I must go back. I mustn't be away for long."

"Before you run away Miss Jewell, can I ask after your master and your mistress? I know them and they've always been kind to me."

Rebecca shook her head sadly. "They're not well, and the mistress forgets a lot. That's why I'm here. She sends me over with little messages which never make much sense. But your mistress is so good and always sends me back with something, biscuits or bread. She gave me an apple pie today."

"So you're the reason we're all going hungry," he said, his face so serious that she looked startled for a moment, but then she laughed, her green eyes suddenly sparkling.

"I like it here," she said, "I can be happy for a while. Most times I've got no one to talk to, with the mistress the way she is, and the master wasting away and always taking to his bed. And the young master doesn't say much. He's always working and worried about his mother and father I think. But they won't have the doctor near them."

"John Chapman's wife Tamson lives near to where you are at Trevivian. Have you met her yet?"

"I meet her walking in the lane sometimes. She asked me to visit her but I don't like to intrude. I don't know Mr Chapman and I'm not sure if he would want me calling on them."

"Visit with her if she asks you. She'd be company for you and she may be able to help. Ask her to call the doctor to them. They won't fall out with her over it."

Rebecca laughed again. "Thank you," she said. "I think that's what I'll do. But first I must return with this apple pie."

As she hurried away and Matthew resumed his walk with Hercules, he saw Tom Prout step back out of sight in the pig house, and wondered how long he had been standing there watching them.

John Peter came out of the farmhouse to look at his horse.

"He's still walking lame Master. His shoe's not looking worn but I'll remove both front shoes and trim his feet right down. I can check for cuts or stone bruising; see if there's any swelling. I'll fetch some hay from the barn before I make a start. They're running low in the stable."

Entering the barn, he climbed the steps that led up to the hayloft and thought he would tidy it up a little, before taking the horses their feed. Before he had a chance to start on the job, the barn door opened and Tom Prout came running up over the steps to join him.

"What were you and Becky Jewell talking about earlier then Matthew? I saw you with her over by the stable. Asking about me was she?"

Matthew decided that Mrs Peter's handsome nephew needed taking down a peg or two.

"No Tom, she didn't mention you. We were just talking about this and that. Matter of fact, I think she's a bit sweet on me."

"Sweet on you! Why ever would she be sweet on you Weeks? I've got my eye on that girl myself, so you keep away from her. D'you hear me?"

"Well that's funny Tom Prout, 'cause it was me she came over to speak with!"

Matthew's saucy retort brought Tom's clenched fist swinging towards his head, and he twisted around to try to avoid it. But it was too late. Matthew's face took the full force of the blow and as all of his weight shifted to his lame leg, it gave away under him and he fell, unchecked, from the edge of the hayloft, and crashed down onto the stone floor below, right on top of Issy's latest litter of pups as they lay sleeping beside their mother.

Tom looked down over the edge and utter chaos seemed to break out below him. Matthew was groaning and holding his face; trying to struggle to his feet to avoid Issy, who was barking and jumping all around him, while her yelping pups seemed to scatter all over the barn. Clattering down the wooden steps, Tom reached Matthew just as he got to his feet, and just as John Peter and Charlotte ran in through the barn door to see what all the commotion was about.

The lifeless bodies of two pups lay squashed at Matthew's feet, and another was running around him squealing in pain, with one leg held high off the ground. Matthew was staggering around and clutching his jaw. Blood had begun to trickle out from the side of his mouth and he was glaring at Tom as if he could strangle him.

"He fell. He fell from the hayloft, right on top of them. He's killed them and we may as well put this one out of his misery as well. He'll be no use to anyone, limping around like Matthew Weeks here for the rest of his days." And bending down, Tom picked up the lame pup by the scruff of its neck and dangled it in front of John Peter.

He was soon to regret his words, as Matthew turned, snarling at him through bloody teeth, "You leave that dog go. He'll mend!" and grabbing the little animal away with one hand he smashed Tom straight in the face with the other, breaking his nose. Charlotte hadn't spoken a word, but she moved over towards Matthew and sliding her arm around him, guided him across the barn and back into the house, through the connecting door; leaving poor John Peter to take his cousin Tom to his own family home, just two fields away at Rosebenault.

December 1840

"Have you seen Charlotte Matthew? See if you can find her for me. She's gone off somewhere again, leaving me to clear up all these dirty dishes. I don't know what's got into her these past few days."
"I haven't seen her since dinner Mistress, but I'll have a look around."

Tom Prout was cleaning out the pig house and Matthew called over to him. They didn't say much to each other these days, not since they'd come to blows more than a year ago. He'd broken Tom's nose that day, and lost three perfectly good teeth himself.
"Have you seen Charlotte Tom?"
"No. Why? Who wants her?" He walked across to Matthew in the middle of the yard, squaring up to him as usual; hostile as ever.
"The mistress wants her. She's got work for her to do."
"She's in the barn." Tom began to hurry towards the barn door but Matthew, despite his lame leg, was quickly up beside him.
"Well, why didn't you say so in the first place!"

They reached the door together and crashed through it like silly children, both wanting to be the first to tell her she was needed in the house. Charlotte didn't even look up. Sitting on a bale of hay with her skirts up over her knees; her hair loose and all messed up, she was feeding milk to a small puppy from one of the bottles kept for orphan lambs. Two more puppies were clambering all over her, eager for their share of the milk. She had never looked lovelier. The two men stopped in their tracks and then, struck dumb by the vision in front of them, turned to look at one another. Charlotte looked up.

"Well whatever's wrong with you two gawping at each other like that? Makes a change I must say. Come over here and help me with these dogs."

"Where's their mother then? It's her job to feed them, not yours. She was in here this morning. I'll swear to it." Matthew had been in the barn that morning, just to check on the pups, but he wasn't going to say so, not in front of Tom Prout.

"Like as not she's off running wild in the fields with their father, chasing rabbits, that's all they think about these days, never mind their hungry pups."

"Nothing wrong with those two dogs. They're good ratters. Anyway, seems you're wanted back in the house." Tom seemed to have found his voice again.

"Well if you two are such good friends now, you can take on feeding them together. There is another bottle behind the hay bale." And with a saucy smile directed at both young men, she flounced past them and out of the open door without a backward glance.

"May as well finish the job since the milk's here." Matthew bent over, picked up both bottles and turned back to hand one to Tom. But Tom Prout was nowhere to be seen.

April, 1841

The first time that Matthew collapsed, he woke up to find himself lying face down in the muddy track that led up towards his mother's house in Higher Larrick. He tried to struggle to his feet, but felt so weak that he sank back down to the ground in a daze and tried to work out what had happened to him. He was sure he hadn't tripped over anything. It had just felt as though the life was suddenly draining out of his head, and all he could remember after that was the helpless feeling as his legs had given up on their fight to hold him upright.

He'd walked for hours that morning in the drizzly April rain, hoping to reach his old home in time to sit down with his mother and sisters to share their Sunday dinner. They didn't know that he was coming to see them, but it was the knowledge that he was always welcome, that had kept him going as he'd passed Elizabeth Stevens' house, without even a sideways glance. His chest had felt heavy then, remembering the last time he had called there, and how she'd been so excited to tell him that she had a young man, a sailor, and that she hoped to marry him some day.

"Oh Matthew," she'd sighed, grasping his hands in hers. "He's so handsome in his uniform. I think I must be the luckiest girl alive!"

He'd realised then, seeing her so happy to share her news with him, that she'd never thought of him as anything more than a friend; never known how much he'd admired her, and even hoped that one day she would be his bride. He'd said goodbye to his rosy cheeked girl that day, and although he'd had to pass her house whenever he visited his family, he hadn't yet been able to bring himself to call in again to see her. He'd been so unhappy lately. Could this have caused him to collapse in such a manner? It wasn't just Elizabeth. Things had changed so much at Penhale that he wasn't so happy there anymore. Edward Peter and his wife Mary had moved back, a few weeks ago, to live at the farm. Charlotte had been sent away, as they needed her bedroom. Even John Peter had gone away for a while, and a cousin, a Thomas Peter had turned up to stay and help around the farm until John came back.

At least he knew that the mistress thought highly of him. Only that morning she'd told him that he had no need to worry about being asked to leave the farm.
"As long as I'm alive Matthew there'll always be a place for you here," she'd said. *"I rely on you, you know that. Don't know what I'd do without you sometimes. You've seen me through a difficult time; you and young Will and Charlotte as well for that matter."* And she'd bustled off upstairs calling for Mary, but he was sure he'd spotted tears in her eyes. What could be upsetting the mistress? She had her son back home with her again, and her daughter-in-law to help her in the kitchen and with the milking.

He was feeling stronger now and his head seemed to have cleared, so he scrambled up and walked on towards his mother's house. It was at this time of year, eight years before, that his little brother George had died, just after his first birthday. His mother still grieved for George, he knew that, and so he liked to visit her at the end of April each year, just to let her know that he hadn't forgotten. Eliza had been born the following year, but George had a special place in his mother's heart; the only one of her ten children who hadn't survived.

"Matthew! I knew you'd come today. I knew you wouldn't forget! But whatever has happened to you son? You've got blood and dirt on your face and your clothes are filthy. Have you been in a fight? Come into the kitchen and clean yourself up son."

"No mother, there's been no fight. I tripped over a tree root just a little way back down the lane. Dinner's smelling good!" Keen to steer the conversation away from his fall, Matthew walked across the kitchen to the sink and opened the little window above it that looked out onto a small garden. "Where are the girls today? I thought they'd be in for dinner by now."

The girls were his three youngest sisters, Janey, Elizabeth, and Eliza, who, normally, he'd have expected to be there on a Sunday, and make a big fuss over him when he arrived.
At first his mother didn't answer him, and looking around at her, he was startled to see such an anxious expression on her face as she turned her eyes away from his.

"Er….well they should be here soon Matthew. Lizzy and Eliza just walked over to meet Janey this morning. They thought they'd be company for her, on her way back home for dinner. It's not that far, but……..." Her voice trailed away as she looked up and their eyes met.
"Not far? But where did they go to meet her? And why are you looking so, well….. so guilty about it?"
"Son, I'm not happy about this and I know you won't be. We've not seen you for a while to tell you Matthew, but Janey's gone into service. The Webbers have taken her on as a kitchen maid, over at

Trekenner, on their farm. She's settled in there well son, they're good to her."

"But mother, she's still a child. I was fifteen before I left home. Janey's only twelve! William and Hannah were fifteen before they went away, same as me."

"Matthew." Jane Weeks interrupted him. "Janey's thirteen now, not twelve, and I know she's quite young to go into service, but I had no choice son. Times have been hard since your father died and, well, it's one less mouth to feed. You must see that."

Matthew did. His mother hadn't had an easy life with six children still at home when his father died. She'd worked hard for them, earning money by cleaning for anyone who could afford to pay her. They would all have had very different lives if John Weeks hadn't died before his own father, leaving his brother Richard as the only heir to their father's farm.

The door burst open and three shrieking girls almost fell into the room. Matthew winked at his mother to let her know that he understood, and quickly sat on the nearest chair before they all hurled themselves at him in their excitement.

"Matthew you're all muddy. Why is there blood on your face? Have you been in a fight? Oh, no! Now I've got mud on my dress!"

Over dinner they all questioned him as usual, wanting to know what had happened to him in the weeks since they had last seen him. His mother in particular was never satisfied until she'd heard all the latest gossip about the Peter family and their neighbours. Life on

Bodmin Moor, it seemed, held a real fascination for her.

"So why do you think Edward and Mary have come back to Penhale then? Do you think they'll stay this time?"

Dinner was over; they were all sitting around the table drinking tea, and Jane Weeks still wanted to know more about this most recent news from Lower Penhale.

"Well they talk as if they're staying on for a while yet. Penhale will belong to John and Edward Peter one day, once their mother's passed on. I think he's likely come back to keep an eye on the farm, make sure his mother's still well enough to run the place. Master John's a good man and a hard worker, but he'd never be able to run the farm on his own, I'm certain of that."

"So why has John Peter moved out then? Is he not happy to be living with his brother again?" This was from Janey. "I would so love it if all of us could be living together again!"

But Matthew couldn't even begin to imagine what that would be like and began to laugh as he answered her. "He hasn't moved out because of Edward. They get along together well enough. No, I think it was Mary who upset him, taking over his seat on the settle every evening, warming her feet by the fire. He had to sit up at the table with his mother instead, and it was strange how quickly he came down with a very bad cough and decided he needed a good dose of sea air to help clear his chest. He didn't sound that bad to me, but the mistress has a sister living in a cottage on the coast up at Boscastle, and that's where he's gone for a while. Just until he's better."

They were all laughing now, but Jane Weeks suddenly grew serious again. "What of poor Charlotte son? What has become of her?"

"She's ....er... gone over to Tremail as a milkmaid on Digory Hayne's farm." Matthew answered slowly but his mother didn't seem to notice and continued to question him.

"Oh, so you've seen her then son? She's not far away. So what does she make of all this?"

It was Matthew's turn to look shamedfaced and avoid his mother's eyes. "I don't really know what she thinks. I haven't seen her at all since she went to them. We've been busy, and I haven't had time to go calling on anyone, until today that is."
"Matthew Weeks. I can't believe what I'm hearing! That girl's been a good friend to you, and you to her, for three years now. Why, she's not much older than our Janey and she has no family to turn to with her problems. Go and see her son. She'll be glad to know that you haven't all just wiped your hands of her. You can't have been that busy that you couldn't just walk over there of an evening. What's wrong son? I can tell when you're not happy. I'm not your mother for nothing you know."

But Matthew couldn't really explain why he hadn't called to see Charlotte. Thinking about it, he didn't know himself. "Everything's different, that's all," he said. "I've lost Elizabeth to some sailor. Nothing's the same at Penhale, and I don't know if Digory Hayne and his wife would want me turning up at their farm to visit Charlotte."

"Well from what I've heard from you in the past, life on the Hayne's farm is very different to life at Penhale. Mr Hayne's wife is much younger than him, isn't she? And they've three young children running about; not to mention half a dozen servants and farm workers all living there. They'll scarcely notice you. Get yourself up there Matthew, for if you ask me, it's not Elizabeth Stevens you're pining after. Am I right son?"

"No mother," Matthew looked up at her, shocked and surprised. "No, Charlotte's a good friend and I miss talking to her and hearing her singing her silly little songs, but that's all. I reckon the mistress is missing her as well." And he went on to tell them how he thought he'd seen tears in her eyes that morning when she'd spoken of the difficult times that he, Will Cory and Charlotte had helped her through.

Jane Weeks got up from the table and started to clear the dinner dishes away. The girls stayed sitting with Matthew. He would have to leave soon if he was to get back to Penhale at a reasonable hour, and they didn't know when they'd see him again.

The conversation turned to his brothers and sisters. The two eldest, Mary and Richard were married now with families of their own, while John and William were still single and rumoured to be drinking too much and running a bit wild. Hannah, who had just turned nineteen had recently met a young man, an engineer at a mine near Latchley in east Cornwall. By all accounts she was very taken with him. Too soon, it was time for him to leave, and they all saw him off at the door.

"Make sure you go to see Charlotte now," Janey called after him, as he made his way back down the lane. "And watch out for those tree roots!"

Matthew lost no time, and early the following evening, made his way to Digory Hayne's farm at Tremail, intent on seeing Charlotte again for the first time in several weeks. One of the servants, Annie Tremeer, opened the door to him before he had the chance to knock, which he thought was just as well, for he was still in two minds about it all, and was about to turn around and walk away. Before either of them had a chance to speak, twelve year old Thomasine Hayne appear beside Annie, looking breathless and excited. "Matthew Weeks! I thought it was you. I called down to Annie to open the door when I saw you coming in the farm gate. Have you come to see Charlotte? She talks of you all the time!"

"That's true enough. The girl scarcely opens her mouth unless she's speaking about you. She's around here somewhere. Come in Matthew." Mrs Hayne, Thomasine's mother, was laughing as she appeared behind her daughter and her servant. Annie quickly retreated to allow Matthew to enter the house, and as he walked over the threshold he saw Charlotte, standing in the middle of the room. She stood, blushing, awkward and embarrassed to hear her mistress speak about her in that way. But as Matthew started to thank Mrs Hayne for inviting him in, he found himself speechless. In those few short weeks, Charlotte had blossomed into a lovely young woman, and he knew that she would never again remind him of his little sister Janey.

Mid October – end of December 1841

Summer had been good that year to the farmers on Bodmin Moor, but now it was mid-October; winter was fast approaching and the nights drew closer every evening. The wind grew colder as it swept across the moor by day, and howled down the chimney when the Peter family gathered around the fire at night. They hadn't seen as much as they normally did of Matthew that summer. He did his work as well as ever, but then disappeared in the direction of Tremail whenever he had some free time, leaving them to decide between themselves what they thought was going on between him and Charlotte.

It was Sunday morning, the changing weather had turned warm, the wind dropped and Phillipa Peter and her family had gathered together in the mowhay behind the house, making the most of the sunshine. While Mrs Peter and her daughter-in-law sat in the hedge, Edward and John stood discussing the farm, close to where Matthew was chopping wood for the fire, before he went out for the day. John was home again and much happier now, having regained his seat on the settle in the evening. Mary, it seemed, now preferred to sit up at the table with her mother-in-law, where, after they had worked together mending any shirts or trousers needed for the next day, they talked endlessly until bedtime.

"Mrs Peter! Mrs Peter!" They all looked across at the far side of the house as old Elias Bettison suddenly appeared there and came shuffling towards them. Elias was an old man now, but he still worked as a labourer for the Haynes at Tremail, and lived in a little cottage on their farm with his wife Susanah.

"I'm sorry to bring bad news, but it's Thomasine and Charlotte. They've got the smallpox and Mrs Hayne, poor woman, thought that you should know and that maybe you could tell Charlotte's mother!"

Elias sank down into the hedge to sit beside Phillipa Peter. "The doctor had them sent away last night for the sake of the young'uns. They'll be with the pox nurse now, over by Brown Willy."

The axe that Matthew had been wielding clattered down onto the path as he stood staring at old Elias for a few seconds in disbelief. And then, without a word, he turned and ran from them, faster than any of them had ever seen him move before.

It was John who spoke first. "Well, if that don't answer your questions mother, nothing does. It's plain now what's been going on there! He's gone to her. He's run off to see Charlotte."

Mary rounded on him, angry at his apparent lack of concern for the two young girls. "You need to watch what you're saying sometimes John Peter! Those two girls could die from the pox and all you're thinking about is what Matthew's been up to with Charlotte!"

Phillipa Peter had turned as white as a sheet. "I never gave it another thought, but Matthew came back last Sunday saying the girls were poorly. Tired he said; sore throats and sickness. That's why he hasn't been over there this week. Said they had enough to do without him hanging around."

Elias nodded. "Real poorly they were. Then, a couple of days back, my Suzy heard they had these red marks and blisters on their hands and faces. The master sent for the doctor, and when he said it was

91

the smallpox, well, I've never seen such a panic break out. The doctor, he said they had to go away, and the master said he was right and they had to think about the boys, but the mistress, well she was wailing and carrying on. Miss Thomasine was real frightened, but it would have been harder for her if she didn't have Charlotte with her. Always around Charlotte she is, helping her milk the cows, and Charlotte helping her with her reading and writing. Close as peas in a pod. The mistress never seemed to mind. Enough to do with those two boys, and her not a well woman since they came along."

Phillipa Peter didn't answer him. She was badly shaken by the news and lost in her own thoughts. The boys were Thomasine Hayne's twin brothers, Emanuel and Digory. She could remember the day that they came into the world, about five years back. It had almost killed their poor mother, giving birth to those boys and she'd never seemed to get the same strength back as before, not even to this day. When Edward had sent word to Penhale earlier in the year, to say that he was coming back there, with Mary, to live for a while, Phillipa had been delighted. But she had worried about Charlotte. Her son and daughter-in-law would need the bedroom that Charlotte slept in, and they wouldn't need a maid with Mary around to help with the chores. Seeing Mrs Hayne at chapel, looking pale and worn out as usual, she'd told her of her predicament and asked if, perhaps, they needed another maid at Tremail Farm. Ann Hayne had jumped at the chance. Her family all knew Charlotte, meeting up at chapel as they did, as well as over the days of the harvest, and at Christmas time. A maid to help with the milking; a maid they knew and liked; a maid who could read and help her children with their education. It had all seemed heaven sent to her. Simon Baker had been to Tresparrat Post to tell Charlotte's mother that she would in future be in service with the Haynes. He had returned to say that she had no objection to the arrangement and had said nothing more to him on the subject. And so Charlotte had left lower Penhale. Not, it had to be said, without anxiously shedding quite a few tears, but it had all worked out well. Phillipa had seen them all a few times at chapel, and it appeared that they were all more than happy with the situation. Ann had looked much stronger, and a little flush of colour had crept back into her face. But now this had happened, and only the good Lord knew what would become of those poor girls.

"We must pray," she said softly. "We must all go to chapel this afternoon and pray."

Mrs Mudge, the pox nurse as she was known, lived at the foot of Brown Willy, the hill that Mrs Peter had once climbed in her younger days with her husband and their children. Alone in her little cottage she lived out her days, remembering happier times when her husband Samuel and their two children Ellen and young Sam, had lived there with her. Together they'd raised horses, pigs and sheep, as well as doing their best to grow their own vegetables in the poor moorland soil. They'd always made enough to get by and been content, until the time, almost four years past, when they'd all been struck down by smallpox.

She had been the sole survivor. Beside herself with grief, she'd shut herself away in her cottage on the moor, wishing every day that she'd been taken, with her family. Scarred as she was by the pox, and with no one to care for, she wondered why she had been spared, until the day, that driven by necessity she'd taken her pony and trap into Bodmin to get much needed supplies for herself and the few animals that remained on her little settlement.

In Hocking's grocery shop on Mount Folly, Emily Mudge overheard the two women who were being served ahead of her, talking about yet another outbreak of smallpox in the town.

"No sign of it stopping," said one of the women, "People dying every day all over Cornwall and up into Devon too, so they say. First ones I heard of was last year, when poor Mrs Mudge's family, out on Bodmin moor all died of it. 'Tis the little ones I feel for. Dying like flies they are."

The other woman was nodding as she packed the last of her groceries away into her basket.
"Poor little souls. What's needed is somewhere they could go, poor dears, miles away from everyone, so they're not spreading this pox around to their families and neighbours. Though who would want to nurse them I can't imagine!"
"Well there's plenty still alive who've had it m'dear," said the first woman, as they both turned and crossed the shop towards the door, without even a glance in Mrs Mudge's direction.
"'Tis common knowledge you can't catch it twice ...."
Their voices had faded away as they opened the door and stepped out into the busy street.

"Are you alright dearie? Can I help you?" The young woman behind the counter sounded concerned as she questioned her only remaining customer, but then she stood astonished as the woman's ashen face had suddenly broken into a beaming smile when she replied to her.

"As a matter of fact I'm sure you can help me. You see, I'd like you to tell everyone who comes into this shop that Mrs Mudge at Brown Willy, out on Bodmin moor, is willing to nurse some of those poor souls with the smallpox. I've got quite a big cottage, miles away from other folk, and two spare beds since my little ones passed away. It makes perfect sense. I've already had this dreadful disease you see, so I won't get it again. Will you do that for me?"

And so Emily Mudge had left Bodmin that day, a determined woman, but not before she'd spread the word a little further, in the post office, to the butcher, around the corn market and to Mrs Helson in the draper's shop. She knew now what she was going to do with her life. She knew, she thought, why she had been spared, and so she vowed to give the best possible attention to any of the afflicted who were entrusted to her care.

That had all been well over three years earlier, and Emily had been kept busy as a smallpox epidemic, with a very high mortality rate, had raged through the south west of England. She'd cooked for them, mopped fevered brows, and washed or burned their bed sheets as she felt necessary. She'd sat by bedsides around the clock, rejoicing when her patients survived and weeping over them when they died. But this year, 1841, had been different. This year, mercifully, it had seemed that the epidemic was over. Emily had nursed two small children with mild smallpox back to health early in the year, but since then she'd been enjoying a well- deserved rest. And so it was with some despair that she'd come home from Bodmin market that Saturday in October, to find Digory Hayne from Tremail Farm awaiting her return. He had begged her to take in his daughter Thomasine and one of their maids with her, if she had the room. His doctor had said they had smallpox, and his wife, knowing of her reputation, wouldn't hear of them being nursed by anyone other than Mrs Mudge out by Brown Willy. But Emily had needed no persuasion. She'd prayed that the wretched epidemic was over, but if it had returned, then so be it. She was more than willing to look after its victims.

And so that evening, Mr Hayne had returned with his daughter and Charlotte, bringing with him their extra bed clothes, and as many spare sheets as the Hayne's household had managed to muster in such a short time. After helping to take the girls into the cottage and up over the stairs to the bedroom they were to share, he left them, promising that Mrs Mudge would be well rewarded for her care, and to send anything that might be needed during their stay with her.

The girls were quiet but obviously frightened and clinging together, not wanting to be separated, so as soon as Digory Hayne had departed, Emily pushed the two little beds together and settled Thoamsine Hayne and Charlotte Dymond down for the night. The master's daughter and his housemaid slept, fitfully, side by side that night, because they were happier that way, and Emily Mudge made herself a makeshift bed on the floor beside them, so as to be right there whenever she was needed.

It had been a long night, followed by a busy morning, and it was mid-afternoon before Emily sat down for a few minutes to collect her thoughts. She'd spent time earlier in the day, getting better acquainted with Charlotte and Thomasine. Whilst checking their mouths and throats for tiny red spots and inspecting the small number of red blisters on their faces and hands, she found many more inflamed blisters on their lower and upper arms. Now they were asleep, and so she sat at her kitchen table, looking out at the familiar moorland view, watching the scattered sheep and horses as they grazed in the rare October sunlight. In the distance she could see someone, a man, walking quite rapidly in the direction of her cottage. He drew closer and for a few seconds her heart stood still. Her Samuel? Her husband? It couldn't be of course but the likeness was uncanny. It was his slight build, the unruly mop of brown wavy hair, even the limp, for Samuel had walked with a limp for most of his life, after falling from his horse when he was still a boy. The man was almost at her door before it became clear that he wasn't her Samuel. To begin with he was much too young; his face as smooth as a boy's; the limp was different, far more severe, and his eyes were dark; Samuel's had been a pale blue. But still she hurried to open the door to him. She paused though, just for a second or two, awaiting his knock before pulling the door open. So, when no knock came, she cautiously opened it, and realised that she would have had a long wait for him to announce his presence. He was lying on the ground, collapsed or fainted, but thankfully breathing. Managing to drag him in through her door, for there

97

was not much weight to him, she left him on the kitchen floor and went in search of some smelling salts. The strong, foul smell of the salts soon revived him, but he still seemed to be in some sort of a daze, and so she sat him at her kitchen table, while she brewed them both a strong pot of tea. She sat and watched him in silence as he slowly downed the tea and ate a large chunk of the fresh bread she'd baked that morning, topped with a generous helping of her home made blackberry jam.

He bore several slight marks of smallpox on his round, youthful face, and his anxious brown eyes were full of far too much pain. However, the colour began to creep back into his cheeks and the dazed expression began to fade away. He spoke in a soft Cornish voice that melted her heart even further.

"I'm sorry about all of that Mrs Mudge. It only happened to me once before."
"Well you were lucky to reach my doorstep, for if that had happened to you out there in the middle of the moor, the buzzards and crows wouldn't have waited to see if you were dead or alive".
Matthew shuddered. He hadn't thought about it before, and he did spend a lot of time working in the fields and out on the moor, miles from anywhere and most times on his own.

"So what brings you here young man? And your name? I don't even know your name."
"I'm Matthew Weeks, Mrs Mudge. Work at Lower Penhale Farm. I heard from Elias Bettison that Charlotte Dymond and Thomasine Hayne are here with you. He said they had smallpox."

"And you came here to see them. Well I hope you'll be well enough to walk back there later Matthew, and take a message from me, that unless I'm very much mistaken, these girls no more have the smallpox than you have. Charlotte has told me that she's a milkmaid, and Thomasine sometimes helps her with the milking. They have cowpox Matthew, not smallpox. Don't know what that doctor was thinking of, frightening folk like that. They've had no spots at all in their mouths or throats, yet they already have red blisters on their hands, arms and faces."

For a moment she thought she was going to lose him again, for he seemed to have slipped back into a daze, but then he spoke, quite urgently.

"Do they know Mrs Mudge? Have you told them?"

"Of course I have Matthew. And they are in much better spirits for it. Sleeping like babies at the moment. But you could look in on them before you go. I'd like it if they could stay here for a while yet though. The cowpox won't kill them, but those blisters are going to turn ugly and it could take weeks, or even months, before they're properly better. They're going to be very uncomfortable, poor dears. It can take twice as long as smallpox before it leaves them and I'm afraid there will be some scars."

"It's Matthew Weeks. Come to see Charlotte." The sound of a weak little voice and some soft giggling came from the top of the stairs that led up from the kitchen. Thomasine stood on the top stair, huddled up in layers of bedclothes, her hair awry, but she was smiling.

"Thomasine! What are you doing out of bed? You'll wake Charlotte my little one." But Charlotte was already standing beside her, and as Matthew bounded up over the stairs to join them, Emily Mudge was witness to a very happy reunion between her two young patients and a caring young man, who was obviously very fond of them both.

Ann and Digory Hayne agreed to let the girls stay on with Emily for a while, but after two weeks had passed, Thomasine's mother could bear it no longer, and sent her husband out to the cottage at Brown Willy to bring their daughter back home. She was still quite poorly and not a pretty sight, but she'd been fortunate and would soon be well again.

Charlotte, on the other hand, was proving to be more of a problem to the Hayne's household. Apparently she had no family who would want her anywhere near them, let alone nurse her back to health. And she wasn't recovering as quickly as Thomasine. Her strength seemed to have gone from her and most of her spirit with it. Emily thanked God every day that the girl hadn't had the smallpox, for she was sure that she would have died from it. Ann Hayne rode out with her husband one day to see Charlotte, and they agreed that she should stay there to be nursed, as there was really no one at Tremail who could be spared to look after her, and she was certainly not fit enough to carry out her duties as a maid.

It was winter now, and mid-afternoon on a cold but bright Sunday in early December. Matthew was getting ready to leave Emily Mudge's cottage and walk back to Penhale Farm before darkness fell. Charlotte had gone back to her bed, worn out it seemed by Matthew's visit and helping Emily to prepare dinner. She had eaten very little of the mouth-watering chicken and vegetables, and even less of the sweet smelling plum pudding, with Emily's homemade cream.

"I'm worried about her Matthew, and no mistake." Emily spoke in hushed tones in case the girl could hear her. "She usually rallies a little when you're here, but not today. The sores on her arms are almost gone now and she's been lucky with her face; only one little scar and that will fade."

"Maybe when she can work again. Maybe that will help her." Matthew couldn't see what they could do. He could only think that in time Charlotte would, somehow, recover.

"You and me Mathew, we're country folk. When my spirits are low I go for a long walk out there on the moor, and when I come back, more often than not, I'm ready to carry on again. And from the way you talk about your walks on the moor, climbing Roughtor and watching the buzzards fly, I think you most likely feel the same way."

"But Charlotte can't go out for a long walk on the moor Mrs Mudge, or climb Roughtor, she's not strong enough, and anyway, she doesn't really like the moors. I think she's frightened of being too far away from people and of being left out there on her own. I don't think that would help."

"No, not the moor Matthew, or even the countryside; I think it's the sea that Charlotte is pining for. She often talks to me of walks on the cliff tops with her mother, watching the waves crash against the rocks in wild weather. I think it's in her blood somehow, the sea and the sand and the fishing. She needs to go back there Matthew."

"Well, her mother won't have her, so I don't see how she could go back. She has no other family there that I know of." Matthew couldn't bear to think of Charlotte going away. It had been hard enough when she'd left Penhale and gone into service with the Haynes.

"I wasn't thinking of her going back there to live Matthew, just going back to be near the sea for a while, walk on the cliff tops, taste the salt in the air as she says. I haven't said anything of it to her yet, but I thought I could take her next Sunday. I have the pony and trap, and if the weather's not too bad, we could go to Port Isaac or Boscastle. It would take several hours to get there I know, but it could be a turning point for her Matthew. And I thought you could come with us. Charlotte would be happier if you came with us."

The following Sunday morning at daybreak, Emily Mudge looked out of her bedroom window to see that the moor was covered in a deep frost. It sparkled in the glow of dawn, in places a pale pink, reflecting the deeper pink of the morning sky. It would be a fine day. She dressed quickly and went to wake Charlotte. Together they wasted no time, cooking eggs for their breakfast and packing two baskets to the brim with pasties, fruit and drinks, to sustain them throughout the long day ahead. Emily went outside to feed her animals and prepare the pony and trap ready for their journey. The day was still bitterly cold but she stood for a while, scanning the moor, hoping to see Matthew making his way towards her cottage, hoping he wouldn't be late arriving. He was there, in the distance, waving when he saw her. She waved back and hurried inside to find warm clothing and blankets to wrap around Charlotte, to protect her from the chill of the day. God forbid that the girl should fall ill again from the cold. This outing was meant to set her on the road to recovery.

The journey wasn't an easy one, with Matthew and at times Emily as well, walking part of the way, especially when they had to journey uphill. This they did to save the pony's legs, leaving only Charlotte to be pulled along in the small trap.

Emily had chosen Port Isaac as their destination, as what was left of her late husband's family lived there. She had visited them with him several times in her younger days and so knew her way around the area quite well.

Leaving the pony and trap in the care of a friendly landlord at the inn nearest to the beach, they made their way to the cliff tops, heavily laden with the blankets and baskets of food, supporting Charlotte between them. It was a little warmer now, the sea calm and the sky a clear blue. Sitting on one of the blankets, they wrapped the other around their backs and sat, huddled together for warmth, Charlotte in the middle. She was quiet at first, seeming tired and content to just gaze out at the ocean, but then Emily suggested that they should eat and unpacked one of the baskets, handing out the pasties which she had made the day before. The tasty treat soon revived their spirits, and Charlotte began to talk, through mouthfuls of meat and potato, of times long gone when she had travelled to Boscastle to walk on the beach, and along the top of the cliffs with her mother.

"Once we took Henry and Sarah," she said, "two of the children who came to my mother's school. That was one of the best days. But the best day of all was when we went to Trevalga, to the inn, to visit my grandmother. When we arrived the fish were in and there were people running about everywhere. I remember them saying that the fish had come in the night before and that all of the fishermen were still out in their boats. It had taken them all night to surround the fish in their big nets and bring them into the shallow water. We ran down to watch. On the way we saw carts full with baskets of fish and people loading panniers with fish for their donkeys and ponies to carry. When we got down to where the fish were all trapped and jumping about in the water, one of the barmaids from the inn was there, digging them out with a spade and sliding them off into baskets. I helped her to carry some of the baskets back up to a cellar and people were piling the fish up into layers and covering them with salt. I was so tired that day, but they were all still working away when we left them to go back home. The barmaid filled my apron pockets with fish and we took them back for breakfast in the morning. They tasted so good. I'm sure I can taste them right now."

Emily laughed at her. "It's not pilchards you're tasting my girl, just the sea salt in the air! But those people would have stayed there working with the fish for days and nights on end Charlotte. They have to salt it and store it all away so that it keeps fresh for months. It's catching those pilchards that earns the fishermen most of their money for the year. They all get their share of the catch. I've seen it too, right here at Port Isaac. There were men up here on the top of these cliffs, signalling to the fishermen, pointing with little bushes in their hands, to show them where the fish were. And the men in the boats were shouting and rowing out to sea. I helped one of Samuel's cousins pile the pilchards into baskets and ...."

"Bet you two both stank of fish by the end of the day!" Matthew interrupted her, not seeming too impressed by it all.

Emily passed him one of the apples she'd packed in her second basket. "You're wrong there Matthew. Well I didn't smell of fish anyway. They were fresh out of the water, still living, not really smelling at all."

"Well they certainly stink when they're spread on the fields. I've been there when that's been done!"

Emily laughed but Charlotte was silent, her head resting on Matthews shoulder, her eyes shut, a little smile playing around her lips.

"I'm not sleeping," she said before they could ask. "Just resting my eyes. I'm still listening."

"Listening?" asked Matthew. "Listening to what?"

"Just to the sea," she replied. "And to the gulls."

And so they sat in silence for a while, watching and listening, as the sea lapped gently against the rocks, and the gulls screamed to each other as they wheeled about overhead.

It was Emily who saw them first. She'd been gazing out at the ocean, thinking about her husband and children and how they would have loved to have been there with her, when she saw a large, dark shadow in the water. As she watched, the shadow slowly drew closer and little flecks of silver, gleaming in the thin sunlight, flickered about above it.

"Charlotte, Matthew. It's the fish! Open your eyes Charlotte. Look. The fish are coming in." And as she spoke they could all see little silver fish, leaping on top of the water, as the huge shoal of pilchards swam towards the shore.

"I didn't know the fish came in December. What are they doing here?" Charlotte couldn't believe her eyes.
"Well in the old days they fished for pilchards from mid-summer through to December. But now they seem to stop watching for them after October."

With no nets to trap them the fish didn't come any closer, preferring to stay out in deeper water, basking in the winter sunshine. It was Charlotte, suddenly feeling a real chill in the air again, who suggested that they should leave.
"We don't want to be going back across the moor in the dark. If you'll help me I'll try and walk up that hill. Save the poor pony's legs. You're both such good friends to me. I'll never forget today. It's been one of the best. I'll get better now I promise." *And get better she did.*

The following Saturday, Emily Mudge and Charlotte made the journey into Bodmin market to once more stock up on provisions. Not wanting to be left alone out in the cottage on the moor, Charlotte had suggested that if she found the outing too tiring, she would call in and visit with Mrs Helson in the draper's shop. She had been to Bodmin market several times with Mrs Peter since that first Saturday, now almost three years ago, when she had seen her mother, framed in the doorway of Mrs Helson's shop, with a knife at her throat. That shocking memory had faded now, replaced by more recent memories of warm welcomes and entertaining exchanges of idle gossip, as Mrs Peter had always made a point of taking her along whenever she called in to see her old friend.

Charlotte was fifteen now and although Emily was more than twice her age, they had grown close over the recent weeks and so walked around the market place, talking and laughing together like sisters. It greatly amused Emily at first, although she said nothing of it to Charlotte, to observe the admiration that her young friend was receiving from so many of the men folk, both young and old. Those without women folk by their side, sometimes stood just watching her while she drew close or passed them by. Fortunately, the girl didn't really seem to notice any of this. Her attention was centred on the pretty things offered for sale on some of the stalls; handbags and lacy gloves; handkerchiefs and necklaces were all coveted and reluctantly replaced. And it crossed Emily's mind, unexpectedly making her feel uneasy, that most of the men folk in the market that day would have willingly bought Charlotte those pretty things, just to have her walking by their side.

"Charlotte, Charlotte Dymond. It is you! Oh my dear it is good to see you, and looking so well!

You see John I said it was Charlotte. We were so happy when we heard that you didn't have the smallpox, weren't we John?" A fair haired young woman had suddenly appeared from behind them, breathless and smiling, accompanied by a man who Emily instantly recognised. It was John Chapman, the butcher who lived at Trevivian. So this young woman had to be his wife. Introductions were quickly made, with Tamson Chapman praising and thanking Emily for looking after Charlotte so well throughout her illness.

"You must come to see us again soon. Come at Christmas. My sister will be staying with us for a while. You haven't met her yet have you?" Tamson turned to Emily. "Charlotte used to visit with me sometimes on Sundays after chapel. And I'd be happy if you could call on me Mrs Mudge. I get quite lonely. John is so busy that he is hardly ever at home. I come from a big family, you see, and I never felt lonely as my parent's house always seemed to be full of our friends. You'll both be welcomed, anytime." And, still smiling at them, Tamson caught hold of her husband's arm and they both turned to make their way back up through the street. It was Emily though who caught John Chapman, turning his head around briefly to look at Charlotte, in the same way that he had been watching her throughout the entire conversation, with, Emily thought, a little more than admiration in his eyes.

The week before Christmas saw Charlotte back on the farm at Tremail, helping to prepare for the festivities. She'd been happy to return to the busy household again, but often found herself thinking and worrying about Emily, only three years older than Mary Westlake, but living all alone and miles away from everyone that she knew, out in her cottage on Bodmin moor.

Sunday 3rd April 1842

Matthew walked towards the Hayne's farm at Tremail on Sunday April 3rd 1842, looking and feeling like a new man. He wore a new dark velvet frock coat, a clean shirt, and dark trousers freshly washed and ironed, and concealed in the inside pocket of his new coat he carried a precious little gift, wrapped up in a pocket handkerchief. On Saturday the 26th March he had received from his uncle Richard a princely sum of five pounds eleven shillings and one penny. The money had been left to him by his grandfather John Weeks, and since it was as much as he could earn on the farm in a quarter of a year, he felt that he could at last better himself and make plans for the future, a future that would, he hoped, include Charlotte Dymond.

She opened the door to him that morning, wearing her best dress, a pretty blue gown which she kept for wearing on Sundays. They had made a plan earlier in the week to go for a walk that day, before morning chapel, and so she was holding her Sunday bonnet and a little blue bag that Matthew had watched her make for herself one evening back in the winter.

"Why Matthew, you're wearing a new coat! Wherever did you find it? And it's made out of velvet!"
"I didn't find it Charlotte," he replied quietly, after she had shut the door behind her. "I bought it yesterday at Bodmin market when I went over with John Peter".
"But how could you afford to buy that coat? Have you come into some money?" She was laughing and clearly didn't believe that he had bought himself such a fine garment.

"Well, be patient and I will tell you. But not until we've walked a little way from the farm. I don't want everyone knowing my business." And so, as soon as Matthew was sure that there was no one around to overhear them, he began to tell her of his good fortune.

"Do you remember my telling you that my uncle Richard inherited my grandfather's farm as my father, who would have inherited with him, had died two years earlier?"

"Of course I do. It was when we climbed to the top of Roughtor together for the first time."

"Well my grandfather did leave some money, to be divided between all of my father's children, and given to us if we lived to twenty-one years, or if we married before that."

"But you reached twenty-one last November. Have you had this money for months and not told anyone?"

"I was only given it two Saturdays ago. My uncle said these things take time. And I have hidden most of it where it will never be discovered. Mrs Peter knows that I have got a little money from my grandfather's estate, but I have asked her not to tell anyone, especially not the master, as I don't think that he could keep it to himself."

"So why then Matthew Weeks, are you telling me? How do you know that I will keep it to myself?"

"Because I love you Charlotte Dymond, and I think that you love me in return. Sometimes I imagine that we are married, and we find work together on a farm where we have our own cottage, like old Elias and his wife. But we wouldn't always have to be servants Charlotte. I could set up on my own as a carpenter or a blacksmith. There will be more money one day from my grandfather's estate. He owned the house that my mother lives in now with my sisters, and it's written in his will that when the house is sold, the money is to be divided up between all of my father's children that are still alive. Though I pray that day won't be with us for many more years. Can we tell everyone that we are courting Charlotte?"

"I think I've always loved you Matthew," she replied softly, "since my first day at Penhale, when you stopped my crying with your hand shadows on the kitchen wall. But then I loved you as I might have loved a brother. But that changed last year. It changed in a single moment when we sat on the cliff top at Port Isaac, and I rested my head on your shoulder to listen to the sea. I knew then that I wanted it to always be like that, with us together, side by side."

"And your head resting on my shoulder." He laughed and pulling her towards him, kissed her gently.

"Matthew, can we tell everyone today that we are keeping company? After chapel? I can't wait to see their faces!"

"We'll tell them," he said. Sometimes he forgot that she was still only fifteen years old. "But first I have a gift for you," and from the inside pocket of his new velvet coat he pulled out his handkerchief and carefully unwrapped a beautiful little coral necklace.

"Oh Matthew, it's lovely. Is it really for me? Did you buy it in Bodmin yesterday?" She was looking so happy, turning the little beads over and over in her hand.

"I walked up to Halworthy Inn one evening in the week," he told her. "I bought it there. I know a little blind girl who lives in Halworthy with her mother. On fine evenings they sit outside in the yard at the back

111

of the inn and try to sell little things that people don't need anymore; and if they sell anything, well, the people give them some of the money back to keep for themselves. The inn is always busy, so they manage to earn enough to keep themselves out of the workhouse. The girl's father died years ago out at sea on a merchant ship. The necklaces and bracelets that they sell are made by a neighbour of theirs, the wife of a second officer, who sails to foreign countries on board a schooner owned by a timber merchant from Padstow. Her husband brings her back little beads, precious stones and sea shells from the countries that he visits. And no two things that she makes are exactly the same."

"Well I love it. Tamson Chapman sometimes wears a coral bracelet and I've always admired it."

"I've noticed. That's why I knew you'd be pleased with it. Now turn around while I fasten it around your neck."

With their arms wrapped around each other, they made plans for their future together and wandered the lanes around Tremail, until it was time to go to chapel.

End of August, 1842

Another harvest supper was well underway in the barn at Penhale, but Edward Peter sat alone in the farmhouse kitchen, his head buried in his hands. His wife Mary was expecting their first child in a few weeks. All the noise and excitement of the celebration had been a little too much for her, and they had returned to the house so that she could rest upstairs in bed.

They had been living at Penhale for a year and a half now, but Mary wanted to go back to her parents farm in St Breward for the birth of their baby. She wanted to be with her family again and he understood that. He had been happy when they lived there together before and he knew that he would be again. It was just that he loved Lower Penhale. The farm had been left to him and to John by their father, and one day he hoped to return there to live with Mary to bring up their children, as he had been brought up, living on the edge of Bodmin Moor.

The door opened and to Edward's surprise, Digory Hayne walked in, looking concerned.
"I heard that Mary wasn't well. I wanted a word with you, but if she's poorly we could leave it to another day."
"She's tired that's all. Sit down Mr Hayne, I could do with some company. And now is as good a time as any to talk. What can I do for you?"
"Well, Mrs Hayne heard that you were leaving and she thought that with Mary gone, your mother might be in need of a maid again."

"Well, she did say that she would have to look for someone soon. Why Mr Hayne? Do you know of a maid who is in need of the work?"

"Not exactly Edward, but Mrs Hayne was wondering if your mother could take Charlotte on again, come Michaelmass or even before if it's convenient to her."

"Charlotte? Are you not happy now with Charlotte? Mother's always said that she's a hard worker and that your children seemed fond of her."

"Well this is it really Edward. We're all fond of Charlotte, but I've got two young male servants who are a bit too keen on her at the moment, both taken a shine to her so to speak, and it's causing unrest Edward, getting in the way of their work. It's not the girl's fault you understand, though she can be a bit too friendly with them at times. But she's keeping company with Matthew I believe, has been for a few months, so we thought it might be easier all round if she came back to Lower Penhale; if you know what I'm saying."

Edward laughed. "Well we haven't got as many young male servants as you have Mr Hayne. Only Matthew and young Will Cory, so I don't think there'll be a problem here. I'll have a word with mother later. Now have a drink with me. I'm sure John hasn't taken it all out to the barn. No, here we are. I'm drowning my sorrows tonight Mr Hayne. Don't want to leave Penhale you see, but it looks now as if my leaving may well be of some benefit to you and yours, so let's drink to that!"

Spring 1843

When William Gard strode out, on Sundays, across Bodmin Moor, it could have been said of him that he was usually bristling with enthusiasm. Now in his mid-forties, he had been a Methodist preacher for most of his adult life, and he was well known for his unwavering faith, and his burning ambition to raise the standard of humanity. His sermons were preached with such zeal that people flocked from miles around to listen to his words; words with which he endeavoured to kindle a spirit of generosity between all people, rich or poor, labourers and criminals alike.

He was by trade a cooper, and employed during the week for his practical skills, making churns and barrels, cart wheels and all manner of tubs and boxes. He was also a confirmed bachelor, living on his own in the parish of Forrabury, spending his evenings writing new sermons and praying for his flock. A flock who were, unfortunately, causing him more concern with each passing week. Only a short time ago, services were held on a Sunday in a variety of places, from small purpose built chapels to farm house parlours and converted cottages. Stalwart preachers would walk miles to deliver their message to eager chapel-goers, who often filled their chosen place of worship to the point of overflowing. More recently however, the congregations had dwindled drastically, to the point where the ever zealous ministers were sometimes preaching to a handful of people who looked as if they had come along purely out of a sense of duty.

And so, on the afternoon of the first Sunday in April 1843, William Gard strode out across the moor in the direction of Tremail Chapel, his emotions in turmoil. He had been unable to decide on a sermon to be preached to the handful of faithful followers who would, he hoped, be gathered together there to greet him. It was this diminished congregation at Tremail that puzzled him most of all. The chapel was new, completed less than four years earlier, and the people who generally assembled there, were in the most part, hard-working, God fearing people who had seemed to take great pleasure in coming together to worship, listen to the sermons and then linger on, outside of the chapel, chewing over their problems and generally engaging in idle conversation.

His heart quickened its pace a little as he reached Tremail chapel and saw more people than usual assembling outside in the lane. Digory Hayne and his family were all there. Elias and Susanah Bettison had come along with them, as well as one of their servants Annie Tremeer. This was to be expected though as it was Mr Hayne who had donated the land for the chapel to be built. William Hocking from Trevivian stood talking to Isaac Cory, who was there with his wife. This was surprising, as Cory usually attended Davidstow church.

Richard Pethick from Tresinney was dismounting from his horse and raised his hand to greet William. The young man was the son of his good friend Abraham, who he had planned to visit on his way back to Forrabury. Richard often turned up at the various chapels in the vicinity of the moor, as it was his practice to attend a service, and then check on his cattle before returning home. Several members of the Peter household were the last to join his little congregation, with John Peter out in front, followed by his mother, his sister Mary and their young maid Charlotte, with a pretty red shawl wrapped around her shoulders. A red shawl! A message from his Lord! In that moment he knew what he was going to share with his flock that afternoon. Not his usual sermon, but a story. The true story both of courage and of serving their fellow man. A story told to him by his own dear grandmother, and directly connected to the building of a meeting house for the members of the United Methodist Free Church, in the parish of Forrabury.

"I am delighted to see so many of you here today," he told them when they were all assembled and seated inside, "and as a result of this I would like to hold the service as usual, but replace my sermon with an inspiring story which involved a member of my own family. And when you have heard it, I would like you all to return to your homes and see if you can uncover a similar story, which has been handed down within your own family. I would be proud to tell your stories to the congregation when next you return to the chapel. Or, if you so wish, you can stand here in my place and tell your story for yourself."

And so he stood and related a tale of a time when this great country of ours was at war with the French, and a Cornish merchant ship was being chased by a French privateer. They were spotted off the coast, from the harbour at Boscastle. Our ship was in grave danger of being caught and claimed as a prize of war, but her captain was familiar with the dangerous coast of north Cornwall, and somehow managed to manoeuvre her around and behind the locally well-known Meachard rock, so obscuring her from the view of the French ship. Word was spreading quickly on

117

land and as the French lowered a boat into the water to search for the Cornish ship, a group of courageous local women came up with a plan to save it, along with the lives of its crew. As the boat was nearing the rock, the men on board saw a long line of red along the coast, and, believing it to be the British army, quickly turned the boat around to go back to the privateer, which itself soon disappeared back out to sea. What they had believed to be a line of British redcoat soldiers was in reality, a line of local women, wearing their red shawls, which were very popular amongst them at the time. They had succeeded in frightening away the French and saving a ship belonging to a Mr Rosevear, a merchant who came from Camelford. His ship, its crew and a valuable cargo had escaped their enemies, and so grateful was Mr Rosevear, that he made up his mind to build a chapel, a United Methodist Free Church, to thank the good Lord for his mercy.

"And," William Gard finished proudly, "my own dear grandmother was amongst those women that day, and her story, and that of her brave neighbours, will be passed down from generation to generation, and held up amongst our people as a noble example of how to serve your fellow men."

His congregation was silent, all awake and seeming to want more from him.
"So," he happily continued, "that is my story. And I hope that some of you will come back to me with your own stories. You may indeed have already thought of something that you could tell us."

To his surprise, the young maid Charlotte, whose pretty red shawl had been his inspiration that

118

afternoon, was somewhat nervously, getting to her feet.

"I have a story sir," she said. "Not one handed down by my own family, but I would like you to tell it for me, maybe at our next service."

"Gladly young woman," he replied, faintly surprised by the delicate way in which she spoke. "May I ask what it is about?"

"It's Emily Mudge's story sir. She lives out by Brown Willy in a cottage on her own. Her husband and children died of smallpox, but she survived. Since then she has been serving her fellow man sir, nursing many people with the smallpox, in the hope that it won't be spread to the others in their households."

Digory Hayne also rose to his feet. "I'd be glad to help you with this story Mr Gard, as would my daughter Thomasine. Maybe if Charlotte can stay on with us for a while after the service, we could tell you what we know about Mrs Mudge.

And so it was a much more contented William Gard who strode back across the moor in the direction of Forrabury that afternoon.

He had scattered a few seeds amongst his flock; seeds that he hoped would sprout and grow, encouraging the congregations back into their chapels to share inspiring stories with their friends and neighbours.

On the following Tuesday morning, as John Peter was crossing the yard on his way to the stable, he was surprised to see Richard Pethick riding in towards the farm. The youngster dismounted and tethered up his sturdy grey horse before entering the yard.

"Is something wrong lad?" John asked as Richard approached him. They were cousins, related on his mother's side, but as John was some twenty years his senior and they lived in different parishes, some eight miles apart, their paths rarely crossed unless it was at market or at the chapel.

"Well, yes in a way. I've come with a message for Matthew Weeks. Is he here?"
"He's out in the fields somewhere this morning, but come indoors and see mother. She'll have spotted you by now and I'll wager she'll have tea already brewing in the pot!"
"I didn't know that you knew Matthew." Phillipa Peter was always delighted to have visitors, but this one was special. Richard hadn't been to the farm since he was a boy and she was eager to get better acquainted with him. She hadn't seen his mother, she realised, for more than a year and they'd always got on so well together in their younger days. But now Richard was here, supping her tea at her kitchen table and wanting to speak to Matthew!

"I don't know Matthew," he replied, "but I've got a message for him from Mrs Mudge."
"Mrs Mudge? From Brown Willy? I know he goes out to see her sometimes on a Sunday, when he's out on the moors. Keeps an eye on her since she nursed Charlotte and Thomasine out there, some while back now."
"Well that's the problem. You see she's not out there now. She's in Bodmin with the doctor, and his housekeeper's looking after her. She kept on at me you see to tell Matthew not to walk out all that way to see her, since she wouldn't be there would she? But she wasn't making much sense poor woman.

Delirious she was. Telling the doctor that she wasn't going with him as he didn't know cowpox from smallpox and she'd be alright looking after herself."

"Richard dear boy, I'm not making much sense of all this. I know we talked about Mrs Mudge and her story at chapel on Sunday, but you've lost me now. Can you start again? From the beginning."

"Well that's it you see. Everyone was talking about her on Sunday with Mr Gard, so when father asked me to ride over to Blisland yesterday; you know we've got land there?" Mrs Peter nodded.
"Well I thought I'd look in to see her as I was riding so close, tell her what Charlotte and Mr Hayne were going to do with her story. I thought she'd like to know. But when I got there, she didn't answer the door and she wasn't around outside anywhere. Her pony was there though, in its little stable, so I knew she hadn't gone far. I opened her door and called out, and that's when I heard her; coughing and gasping for breath she was. So I called out again, but she said that I was to go away. *"I'm ill,"* she was saying.
"Best you go away". But I told her I was coming up to see her. Well I couldn't ride off and leave her could I? Not with her looking after folk the way she does. Well she was real poorly. Coughing and croaking and off her head a bit. I told her I'd get the doctor, but she said he was no good and I should go about my business. But then she asked if I could just feed her animals for her. So I went down and saw to them, and then rode off into Bodmin for the doctor. I thought she had something like bronchitis you see. I'd seen father with it and I knew she wouldn't get better without someone to look after her. Round the clock we had to look after father; had to keep him propped up in bed

and keep his temperature down. Well anyway, Doctor Jenkins came back out with me. Brought his pony and trap. He said I was right; she wouldn't get better without nursing and that he was taking her to his house; and his housekeeper would watch over her until she was better. She wasn't having it at first but she wasn't well enough to do much about it, so we dressed her up warm and he took her back off into Bodmin. I called in to see Mr Hayne just now, and he says he'll make sure her animals are cared for. So I just need to see Matthew and give him her message."

Well Richard, I think you've got your own story to tell in chapel now." Mrs Peter topped up his tea and sat down with him again. "But we'll give Matthew the message for you. Now stay a while and tell me about the family. The youngster could certainly talk, but he was proving to be good company, and she was wanting to hear all about his mother and his older sisters and brothers.

Much later she walked out into the yard with him, just to wave him on his way, but seeing that Charlotte was there, stroking the nose of his grey horse, she said her goodbyes and went back in to clear away the cups. That girl did love horses. No doubt he'd be there for quite a while, and she could watch them from the windows as she went about her work. Charlotte would want to hear all about what had happened with Mrs Mudge. She'd have to have a word with the girl though, holding on to Richards arm, and planting a little kiss on his cheek like that, when she hardly knew him. She'd be heading for trouble if she carried on like that with the men folk. Poor Richard had gone quite red in the face. And what would Matthew have thought if he'd seen it?

Mid-April 1843

Thomas was working in the upper room of the barn, just tidying up the hay bales. He was looking forward to going to the farmhouse kitchen, for a warming cup of tea by the fire. He could hear Charlotte out in the yard, calling for the dog that she had named Charlie; the little terrier that had been injured three years before, when Matthew had fallen from the hayloft and landed right on top of Issy's litter of pups. The barn door opened and the girl walked in, still calling and looking around for the dog.

"He's not here Charlotte. Aven't seen him all morning."

"Tom Prout! You startled me. What are you doing here again? I thought you were working over at Helset now." She went over to sit down on one of the bales of hay that he'd just thrown down to feed the bullocks.

"I like it here at Penhale," he'd said, running down over the wooden steps to sit on the other hay bale beside her. "I'd come and live here like a shot if Matthew moved out."

"Why don't you two like each other?" she asked him.
"Matthew won't tell me. He says it's nothing. Just that you two took a dislike to each other when you worked together on a farm in Lezant. No reason for it he says; just that you never got on."

"Trecarrell Farm," Tom nodded, "that's where we both worked for a while, about eight years back. Matthew was living there, labouring, along with his brother Richard. Word was that Thomas Batters, who owned the farm was a good friend of their grandfather, John Weeks. Richard Weeks was my age but Matthew wasn't much more than a boy, around fourteen I'd say. It was when Richard Weeks left the farm, went back home because his father was ill, that Thomas

Batters took me on in his place. Matthew's right Charlotte. It was nothing really. We just never got on."

"Nothing really! Nothing really! Come on Tom. I've seen the way you two are around each other. And there's the little matter of a broken nose and three missing teeth. Something must have gone on between you!"

"Well it was mostly my doing if you must know Charlotte. I got the wrong end of the stick on my first day working there, and had words with Matthew about something he'd had nothing to do with."

"Nothing to do with! Wrong end of the stick! Spit it out Tom Prout.

What happened that day?"

"Well I didn't know any of the other men there, but when they first clapped eyes on me they were joking about, laughing together, saying *'Weeks was right, he is a handsome bugger. Weeks said the women folk couldn't keep their hands off him. We'd better lock up our women.'* I just laughed along with them. I didn't want to make enemies on my first day there."

"But when you met Matthew," Charlotte interrupted him, covering her face with her hands, "you thought he was the one who'd been saying these things about you."

"I heard someone call him Weeks, and when I got him on his own I threatened him. Told him that he didn't know me and he was to shut his mouth and not to speak about me again to anyone."

"And afterwards you found out that it was Richard Weeks who'd been saying these things, not Matthew."

Tom nodded. "Richard Weeks did know me. We'd met up a few times, harvesting together as youngsters. And well, after that Matthew couldn't take to me nor

124

me to him. We did talk about it, sorted it out, but it was too late."

"Is that all it was?" Charlotte shook her head in disbelief, but then she laughed. "And anyway, he was only telling the truth wasn't he Tom? You are a handsome bugger. Richard Weeks told the truth, and I'll wager he was right about the women folk as well Tom Prout. I'll wager they still can't keep their hands off you. Even with that broken nose. Am I right?" And she reached out, teasing him, tracing her finger down across his nose to his lips.

He drew back startled. "Now you stop that Charlotte. You're walking out with Matthew, so you mind what you are doing with me. I saw you in the yard a while back making up to poor Richard Pethick like this. You'll get yourself into trouble girl, teasing the likes of me behind Matthews back. I saw young Pethick's face. He didn't know what to do with himself."

"Richard's just a boy Tom. He's way too young for me. It was just a bit of fun."

"And I'm way too old for you, young woman. There must be twelve years between us and you only just turned sixteen."

"I'm sorry Tom. I don't know what comes over me sometimes. I don't mean any harm. The mistress is always telling me to watch myself and stay out of trouble. She warns Matthew as well. Says we are both heading for trouble."

"What you're missing is a mother to teach you right from wrong. It's not your fault Charlotte. But just you mind what I've been saying. You'd better get back to the house before you're missed. Don't look like you're going to find Charlie around here," and he left her, running back up the wooden steps to his work. Better not to stop for that cup of tea, he thought to himself. At least not today.

Summer 1843

It was one morning at the end of June that Phillipa Peter saw old Elias Bettison approaching her door. He'd been calling around quite often recently, bringing them news of a teetotal festival that was to be held at Roughtor on the 4th July.

"I've no time for this teetotal nonsense," he'd told her, *"where's the harm in having a beer with your neighbours at the end of a day's work?"*
But nevertheless he had a fascination with the forthcoming festival, and was seeming to enjoy turning up with little snippets of information about it that he'd heard on his travels.
"There'll be a big crowd out there," he'd told the Penhale household when he'd walked in one day as they were all sitting down to their dinner. *"Prayers and singing and bands playing so they say."* On one occasion he'd called around to tell them of plans for banners and speakers at the meeting. On another, that there would be booths set up for the sale of tea and coffee. It was rumoured, or so he'd heard, that there might be an area where local publicans would set up their own booths to sell liquor to anyone who didn't agree with the teetotal nonsense.
"Might take a look out there myself you know," he'd said, when of course they already knew that he wouldn't be able to stay away.
"So what news of the festival today then Elias?" Phillipa asked him as he edged his way in around her door. "Best put that iron down for a minute Charlotte and make Elias here a brew of tea."

Charlotte, who was ironing bedsheets beside the fire, which burned continuously in the large hearth, was only too happy to oblige. The weight of the iron was making her arm ache and she needed a drink herself.

"Oh, I haven't come about the festival, although I did hear that there's to be a wrestling ring out there and donkey racing. No, I've come with news of Mrs Mudge."
He went on to tell them that Digory Hayne had returned from Bodmin the night before saying that Emily Mudge was not coming back to live on the moor. It appeared that Mr Hayne had met up with Doctor Jenkins outside the corn market, and on enquiring about Emily's health, was told that she was much better now, and that she was staying on at his house in Bodmin as his housekeeper. She'd been helping with his patients, he'd said, as well as doing the housework and the cooking, and when he'd told her that he didn't know how he'd manage without her if she ever went back to her home to live, she'd said that she didn't want to live alone out on the moor ever again, and that she would be happy to stay on and work for him if she was needed.

"But what happened to the other housekeeper?" Charlotte asked, "the one who helped to nurse Emily back to health?"
"Well that was the problem you see Charlotte. Mr Hayne was saying that the woman didn't much like being told that she was expected to nurse the doctor's patients as well as run the house for him, and so she left him for a new position over in Wadebridge."

"That was a blessing then, for the doctor, having Emily there; willing to take all that work on," said Mrs Peter, pouring Elias a second cup of tea.

"And a blessing for Emily," said Charlotte. "I was frightened for her sometimes, living out at Brown Willy in her cottage, all on her own."

"But what will she do about her cottage?" asked Mrs Peter, "and her animals? She will have to sell all of her animals surely."

"I don't know about the cottage, but Mr Hayne had us bring the animals to the farm a few weeks back. Said he couldn't really spare one of us going out there on the moor every day, feeding and watering them. He'll likely see her right and give her something for them. He did ask me though to take her pony and trap over to her. Said she'll need to keep them to get about and visit her friends. The doctor's agreed to stable her pony there along with his horse."

"You could visit her from time to time Charlotte," Mrs Peter said, "when we go into Bodmin on market days."

"We'll have so many things to talk about. I haven't seen her in months! Could we go to Bodmin this Saturday, Mistress?"

It was hard to say no to the girl, but Phillipa Peter had other plans. "I wasn't thinking of going anywhere this Saturday, Charlotte. We'll all have a lot of work to do over the next few days if we're having time off for the festival on the 4th."

"Time off mistress? Are we all going out to the festival?" Charlotte looked so shocked that Mrs Peter laughed.

"Well John's been making noises about going, and I overheard Matthew and Will saying they would like to see what's happening out there; so I thought that you would likely want to go alone with Matthew. Of course if you don't want to go, I'm sure I could find something for you to do around here."

"Oh no mistress. I've heard so much about it from Elias. The crowds of people that will be out on the moor, the speakers and the bands playing. I've been wishing that I could go for days now. Thank you mistress."

And Charlotte returned to ironing the bedsheets with fresh vigour, her aching arm forgotten and her mind filled up with vivid visions of the lonely moorland around Roughtor, with scores of people, all laughing and shouting together above the noise made by braying donkeys and the loud music from competing bands.

On the morning of Tuesday the 4th July, a thick mist enveloped the whole of Penhale Farm. The younger members of the household however, were undeterred, and rose early to do the milking and feed the animals.

Will was the first to leave. "I'm off now," he called as he clattered down over the stairs. "Meeting up with father."

"Is your mother not going then Will?" asked Mrs Peter.

"Doubt it. Crowds don't suit Mother." And he was gone; out through the porch and racing off up through the lane as if the devil were after him.

Matthew and Charlotte were ready to go and waiting in the yard when John joined them, and started kicking stones around to pass the time until his mother came out. But Phillipa Peter had had a change of heart. Noticing them all waiting for her outside, she opened the window and called out to them.

"I don't much like this fog," she said, "and the day is far too damp and dirty for me to go traipsing out on the moor, and seeing I'll have no dinner to prepare I might walk up towards Trevilians Gate a bit later, and call on Maria Cory. I'm sure Isaac will be out on Roughtor to watch all of the goings on, but Maria won't be there. Will said she's not one for crowds and I'd like to catch her on her own. There's something I need to talk over with her."

By eleven o'clock the fog was lifting, and since the air was damp and the lanes would be wet underfoot, Phillipa put on a warm shawl and a stout pair of shoes before making her way towards Trevilians Gate. Issac and Maria Cory had moved there from St Breward parish well over twenty years before, to be near family. It was well known that the Peters looked after their own, and as Maria was Digory Prout's sister, she was a sister-in-law, by marriage, to Richard and Phillipa Peter. Since then, Isaac had worked as a farm labourer at Penhale and at Rosebenault, but he had recently acquired three arable fields on the edge of the moorland, and so he was now a small farmer in his own right.

Phillipa almost tripped over the old milk pail which someone had placed on the floor of the little wooden porch way which protected the entrance to the Cory family's kitchen. Hearing the unexpected disturbance, Maria bustled out to the porch to find her sister-in-law in the process of moving the bucket to the side of the door.

"Oh my dear, how good it is to see you! I hope you didn't fall over that blessed bucket. Isaac will insist on putting it there to catch the rainwater. I've said to him as how it would be easier just to get the little roof mended. But well, you know what the men folk are like."

And giving Phillipa a sisterly hug, she bustled back into her spotless and tidy kitchen. Phillipa joined her and crossed the slate floor to stand and warm herself by the small fire which glowed in the open fireplace.

"I'll send Matthew down in the week. He'll fix up that roof for you in no time. No sense in carting pails of water around when we've a perfectly good carpenter on hand!" Phillipa knew that Isaac wasn't as fit as he could be these days. He'd grown quite portly over the past years and she couldn't imagine him scrambling about on the roof of that old porch way.

"Best not mention it to Matthew dear. I don't think Isaac would be too pleased to find him here. You know how it is between those two of late."

"Well I was going to speak with you about this quarrel between them, try to make some sense of it. They are scarcely speaking now as far as I can see, and Matthew walks out of the house whenever Isaac calls in to see me or Will. The best they can manage is to grunt at each other if they meet in the doorway. There's more conversation going on between the pigs out in the piggery. I don't know what I'm going to do about them and that's a fact."

Maria had brought a freshly baked saffron cake and a strong brew of tea to the well-scrubbed kitchen table and Phillipa, now thoroughly warmed through by the fire, sat down gratefully beside her old friend.

"Isaac told me as how Matthew came at him, ranting about some of your young bullocks which he'd had to go after, as they'd wandered off out onto the moor. It seems that Matthew thought that Isaac must have seen them going past him when he was out in his wheat field. Cursing he was, so Isaac told me, asking how he could let valuable beasts pass him by and go out onto the moor to get lost. Well Isaac told him that he hadn't seen any bullocks, and the thing is my dear that I rather think I believe him. Matthew wasn't having any of it, but what he doesn't know, or anybody else for that matter, is that Isaac's eyes aren't what they used to be. Oh, he tells me that he can see well enough and that I'm not to make a fuss about it, but I don't believe he can see very much at all out of his right eye. So I'm afraid Phillipa that he may not have seen your bullocks wandering out onto the moor. He swears so at any rate."

"But this is serious Maria." Phillipa Peter placed her hand comfortingly over that of her sister-in-law. "I'm not meaning this silly quarrel. I can sort that out with Matthew now that I know the truth of it. But if Isaac really is losing his sight, it will be very difficult for you both."

"Well he won't talk to me about it, so we'll just have to face it when the time comes. But if Matthew could tell him that he was sorry for what he said, and they could forget their differences, we may at least be able to get the porch roof mended! Now tell me your news. Have they all gone out to the temperance meeting on the moor? I don't know why Isaac's out there I must say. He's hardly going to turn teetotal is he? With us living next door to a beer house!"

They laughed, but before Phillipa could answer, her sister-in-law spoke again, this time in hushed tones, as if she was afraid of being overheard. "Speaking of Matthew, how are you managing with the young lovers living there together under your roof?"

"There's nothing going on in my house, for I'd not have it my dear, but as to what's going on out in Matthew's woodshed, I can't tell you. Matthew carves these handsome little animals with a special carpentry knife that he bought in Bodmin. He gives them to a little blind girl up at Halworthy and she sells them for him, so he says. Keeps half the money for herself and her mother. But Charlotte's out there in the shed with him most evenings and we can hear them from the yard larking about together. Our Thomas didn't take too kindly to it poor soul, and we don't see so much of him lately. He's always had an eye for Charlotte though he's never said so, and I reckon he could hear them from the pig house. I could see him from my kitchen, crashing about outside like a bull with a sore belly, and hitting the wall with his fist."

Maria frowned. "I thought Tom was seeing Rebecca Jewell a while back. They made a pretty pair."

"Oh I thought you would have known my dear. Rebecca went up to Treglasta to work after poor Edward and Jenefer Hocken passed away. That was a sad business with them both passing within a month of one another. Young William Hocken took it badly, but Rebecca came over to tell me that she didn't feel right about staying on in the house with him on her own. They had no other women servants living in you see. Charlotte missed Rebecca sorely after she left. They'd been good friends, those two girls."

"How's he managing now then? He's got a fair sized house there."

"Matthew told me that Tamson Chapman was going over at first, helping around the house and taking him meals. But it seems John Chapman wasn't happy and put a stop to it, so now Jim Somer's mother is housekeeping for William and he's hiring in a few extra men as labourers on the farm.

"And how do that pair know so much about William Hocken's business then?" asked Maria, still eager to learn more of Matthew and Charlotte.

"Charlotte often visits Tamson Chapman on Sundays after chapel, and Matthew spends a lot of time there with her now, when he's not going to Lezant to see his mother. No doubt they've heard these things from the Chapmans.

The two women sat nattering together for quite a while before Phillipa Peter made her way back to Lower Penhale, happy that she'd got to the bottom of the unpleasantness between Isaac and Matthew, but now more concerned about Isaac's failing sight. She may not have been quite so content with her day however, if she'd known what was happening out at the meeting on the moor.

John Peter had been getting impatient with Charlotte and Matthew's slow progress over the uneven and course moorland grass. Charlotte was wearing pattens to protect her shoes and keep them up off the muddy, wet ground, but the problem was that she wasn't used to walking in them, and her shoes were slipping on the wooden soles.

"You'll do yourself an injury in them things," he told her, "turn your ankle over I shouldn't wonder. I'll make my way on ahead of you. Don't want to miss the start of it."

As it happened, the young couple still made it out to Roughtor in time to see a number of waggons being set up to serve as a platform for the speakers. Hundreds of people were arriving on foot and horseback and in all manner of waggons. It was all just as Charlotte had imagined it would be, and they both joined in with the singing and prayers at the start of the meeting. There were banners flying, and a Lieutenant Dunstan from the Royal Navy spoke from the platform to introduce an energetic speaker who proved to be very successful in rousing the crowd in support of the temperance movement. A band had journeyed out from Bodmin to help raise the spirits of the crowd, and after they had played, another speaker began to scramble up onto the platform, to address the growing number of people who were gathering around the waggons. Charlotte stood in awe of everything that was going on, and would have stayed longer, but Matthew was tiring of it.

"Let's see if we can get a cup of tea or coffee and something to eat," he said, and so they wandered away through the crowd, and soon found the refreshment booths where they bought coffee and pasties.

"I don't see any donkey racing, or a wrestling ring," Charlotte remarked, sounding more than a little disappointed. They had finished their coffee and made their way to where there were a few less people and they could enjoy their pasties without being pushed and jostled by the crowd.

"I wouldn't believe everything old Elias says." Matthew laughed. "He gets a bit carried away at times."

"But there's something going on down by the ford." Charlotte was pointing to a spot several gunshots away, where there seemed to be more booths set up, and another, smaller gathering of people.

"Let's go and see then," Matthew said, "I've had enough of that temperance meeting!"

And as they drew closer, they could see that there were indeed more refreshment booths set up, but that they were being run by local publicans, who were selling very different drinks to the permitted teas and coffees.

"Simon Baker's got a booth over there," whispered Charlotte, and she slipped her arm through Matthew's, as she looked around and found herself surrounded by more than a few unshaven, unwashed ruffians who were already the worse for drink. "And look Matthew, there is a wrestling ring!"

"And look who's there Charlotte. I'll give you a shilling if that isn't Tom Prout in the ring!"
They moved a little closer to watch, standing amongst some unkempt women with untidy dirty hair.
"It's not proper wrestling," Matthew said as they watched Tom in a close hug with a sturdy, barefoot young man. "Simon Baker and his cronies have got together and put this on, to draw the crowd down to their beer booths."

"How do you know that?" asked Charlotte, her eyes fixed on the pair as they clung together, both desperately trying to force the other to the ground.
"They haven't marked out proper rings or tucked up their trousers. Tom's still wearing his boots. And there's only one man to watch them when they fall. There should be three. See there, the man with the stick. He'll raise that when one of them's thrown flat on his back."

The younger man seemed to be tiring as his bare feet slipped, time after time, on the wet grass. Someone shouted from behind them, "Come on Tom, I've got a shilling on you." Another called out "Prout'll win this easy. He only needs one more 'back'"

Almost as he spoke out Tom seemed to lift and throw the other man down. His shoulders and buttocks hit the ground together. The stickler raised his stick and Tom stepped away from the ring as the victor, holding up one arm in triumph, and Matthew could see that he too had been drinking heavily. One of the women standing near to Charlotte called out "Ow about a kiss then darling?" and Tom turned just as the woman landed at his feet, pushed forward by her jeering companions. But he scarcely looked down. He had seen Charlotte and swaying slightly, he stood on one of the shrieking woman's hands as he stepped over her.

"Well look who's here. The belle of Bodmin Moor. Do you have a kiss for me then Charlotte Dymond? A kiss from the belle of Bodmin Moor. Do I deserve that today?"

As he spoke he caught her around the waist and swept her up off her feet, so that her face was level with his. But he didn't kiss her. The haggish women were whistling and calling "Kiss him! Kiss him!" An old man, puffing on a foul clay pipe, nudged Matthew's arm and cackled "This is more sport than the wrestling!" and still Tom held on to Charlotte. She was looking straight into his eyes and he could see that she was hurt and angry with him; so much so, that he suddenly sighed, and relaxing his grip, set her down again gently, but not before he'd rested his head against hers and whispered, "What is the use of it all Charlotte? What is the use of it?"

He turned and moved away from her, back towards the ring.

"Won't she kiss you then darling? Stuck up little madam! Where's the arm' in a little kiss?" The women jeered and hissed and Charlotte glared at them. One of her pattens had fallen off and her bonnet sat sideways on her head. Matthew stood facing her, his face like thunder.

"Have you encouraged him Charlotte? Why would he act like that? And what was he saying to you? I saw him whispering in your ear!"

"He asked me what was the use of it," she replied truthfully, shocked by his anger, for she had done nothing wrong.

"He said more than that. I don't believe you. Tell me what he said!"

The little crowd gathered closer to them. More sport!

"How dare you make a show of me." Charlotte's reply was quiet but cold, almost venomous. "First Tom, and now you. One man who should be my friend and one who would be my lover. How dare you!"

"They would both be your lover dearie. No mistake there!" cackled clay pipe.

"Tis 'er fault my hands broke," whined the woman who had started the whole rumpus. "Belle of Bodmin Moor! Don't look so pretty now do she? With her 'at falling off."

"Leave her be Elsie. She's nothin' to you. The wrestlin's started up again."

With one last scornful glare at Charlotte, Elsie walked away, still nursing her damaged hand. The other women all followed her, along with claypipe. The little crowd soon drifted off, some towards the wrestling ring, but most towards the liquor booths.

Only one man remained, still watching, but unnoticed by either Matthew or Charlotte. She had spotted her lost patten, and limped over to stubbornly and slowly replace it on her now muddy and slippery shoe. Matthew joined her and reached out to untie her bonnet. He took it off, along with her bonnet cap, so that her soft curls fell around her shoulders. His dark expression softened as he tied the bonnet, with the cap tucked inside it, securely onto her arm.

"I'm walking over to Emily's cottage," he said. "You coming with me or staying here?"

She was still angry, her face flushed, but she gathered up her skirt and stomped away beside him. Those ridiculous pattens. How could she walk in them? So his first born had grown up and the stallions were already pawing the ground around her. He wished he could be there to help. Ben Kircher watched as Matthew's arm slid around his daughter's waist and she rested her head against his shoulder. Her bonnet swung on her arm and the little white cap fell out unseen onto the muddy grass. He ran to pick it up before it was trodden into the watery ground and lost forever on the moor. But he didn't go after her. Instead he pushed the cap into his coat pocket, and still holding it tightly in his hand, watched until he could no longer see her blue gown weaving around in the crowd.

"Someone's moving into the cottage." Charlotte stopped walking and tugged at Matthew's arm, pulling him back.

"They won't want us there."

Sometimes he couldn't believe how shy she could be around people that she didn't know well.

"Don't be silly. I want to see who it is. They won't mind stopping to talk for a while."

A large farm cart, well overloaded with furniture, blocked their view of the cottage. A man, a woman and several small children were hurrying to and fro, lifting bits and pieces off the cart and carrying them inside. The man saw them first, and pushing a hefty looking mattress back onto the cart, held out his hand to Matthew.

"Well met young man, young lady. Hezekiah Speare at your service! What brings you to our humble abode? Been at the temperance meeting have you? We've heard the bands playing haven't we my dear?" His wife stood with her hands on her hips, a hostile expression on an otherwise attractive face. She hadn't expected visitors and Caius' would talk the day away if she didn't stop him. She wanted her furniture indoors. While Matthew spoke with her husband, introducing himself and his girlfriend, explaining why they had walked there to see the cottage, she watched the girl, clinging weakly to his arm.

"You must come inside. My wife will make us tea." Caius was ushering them indoors, but Matthew stopped him.

"Why don't we help you unload the cart first, and place the furniture around for you? We'll be happy to do that, won't we Charlotte?"

"You can help Caius unload the cart if you wish young man, and when you've done, you can join me and your girl here for a drink of tea. The girl's all in. Why is it that you men can never see that? Come inside and sit with me my dear, and we'll tell them where to place the furniture!"

It was as they were leaving that Caius issued them the invitation.
"Anytime you are crossing the moor at night," he said, "we'll be glad to put you up here, won't we my dear? You'll be more then welcome."
"And why, may I ask, would these young people be crossing the moor at night Caius? Talk sense will you!" Ann Speare pursed her lips, hands once more resting on her hips. A cup of tea for a helping hand was one thing. Spending the night was quite another! Her name wasn't Emily Mudge, not by a long chalk!

Next morning, breakfast at Penhale farmhouse was taking quite a while longer than was normal. Phillipa Peter sat and listened as John, Will and Matthew each told her about their day out at the festival. Charlotte, she noticed, was unusually quiet and seemed to be nervously watching the door. It was Matthew's story though, that made his mistress sit up and really take notice.
"Hezekiah Speare," she exclaimed, "living out on Brown Willy! But surely he is a shoemaker over in Blisland. Has his own business as far as I know. Whatever has brought him out to live with his wife and small children in a cottage on the moor."
"Fancies himself as a herdsman now," Matthew told her, "needs a change so he says."
"More like his wife who needs the change." John Peter was grinning. "Caius Speare is a mite too fond

of the ladies, or so I've been told. Well he won't be meeting so many of 'em out on the moor will he? Not like he would have over in Blisland making shoes."

"Father! What's this in your pocket? Leading me to believe that you had gone out on business, and now I find a bonnet cap in your coat!" Unity was laughing, teasing him, holding the wet and muddy bit of lace aloft.

It had rained heavily on his journey to their home at Trebarwith and he had been soaked to the skin. Unity had been waiting for him in the kitchen. She'd helped him off with his heavy greatcoat and sent him away upstairs to change into dry clothes, while she'd prepared the supper. His meal was ready on the table when he returned to the warm and welcoming room, and his daughter had obviously searched through his pockets, before hanging his coat up to dry near the fire.

"It's Charlotte's," he said, "your sister's."

"Charlotte's?" she sat down across the table from him, watching him tuck into his food. "You've met with her again then. But why did she give you her bonnet cap? And why is it so muddy?" She was still holding it, rubbing the mud deeper into the cap with her fingers.

"I haven't spoken to her," he explained between mouthfuls. "I did go out on business, but I heard there was a temperance festival out on Bodmin moor and rode over to take a look. I saw Charlotte, just by chance, walking away from me with that crippled boy I told you about. Her bonnet was on her arm and that little cap fell out of it, without her knowing. I picked it

142

up, but not before it had already been stepped into the dirt."

"Why didn't you go after her, give it back? You could have spoken with her again."

Unity knew all about Charlotte. He had told her soon after her mother died, giving birth to their infant son. She knew that she had an older half-sister, and that the girl didn't know that he was her father. She'd been ten years old at the time, and seemed curious, asking questions; but within the month her baby brother had followed his mother to the grave, and they hadn't spoken of Charlotte again, until almost a year ago, when they had returned to Cornwall to live.

Following the deaths of his wife and son, he had thrown himself into his work, breeding horses for the gentry, and his reputation had spread rapidly. He'd been paid well for his fine horses and taken care to look after his earnings. He'd only been eight years old when his own father had died, and it had come as a shock to discover, shortly after his mother had passed away, that the father he could barely remember, had left him, their only child, quite a large sum of money. Enough money to realise his dream, and return with his daughter to the north coast of his favourite county; where he bought himself a house and a few fields, and continued to breed his horses.

It was only then that he had spoken to Unity about Charlotte again.

"I hadn't forgotten," she'd said, "I've been thinking that we might be quite close by to her here, and that I might meet with her one day. We haven't any other family around us now, have we father? Only the two of us and Charlotte."

Now she was smiling across the table to him, holding Charlotte's bonnet cap in her hand. "I'll wash it for you father. I'll clean it up and we'll keep it safe."

He was extremely proud of her. She had grown up travelling the length and breadth of the country, either on foot or on horseback. Her shelter had been a tent, which she'd sometimes carried on her back or pushed in a handcart with their other belongings. There had always been other family members travelling with them, aunts and uncles, cousins, his own mother, until she too had died, more than a year ago. In that year their whole lifestyle had changed. It was just the two of them now, living in a house, running a horse farm, breaking in colts; something which his fifteen year old daughter could do as well as any of the hired men. She hadn't seemed to miss her other family at all, or the travelling, and she really loved the house, keeping it spotless, decorating every nook and cranny with the brightly painted pots, plates, and porcelain figures that she brought back from fairs and market stalls. He teased her, saying that she was spending all of his money, but she always replied that since he didn't buy her gowns or bonnets or necklaces and the like, he had no reason to complain. The truth was that she wasn't interested in wearing them. As a child she'd worn dresses, but, now, working as she did around the farm, she'd taken to wearing trousers and boots, and had even cut her hair to shoulder length, keeping it tied back away from her lovely face. He would have liked to have seen her looking more feminine, but it was enough that she was happy and that they had been able to put down roots in Cornwall, and could wander sometimes, on foot or on horseback, along its sandy beaches and haunting cliff tops.

The following evening Ben noticed Charlotte's bonnet cap drying on the mantle above the fire. Fearful that it may end up in flames, he took it down and placed it on the table. When Unity came in, she picked it up straight away.

"It's still wet. Why did you take it down? Afraid it would fall and be burnt up? I would have dried it out on the bush but I thought the wind might take it. I'll dry it in my bedroom by the open window. Don't worry, I'll make sure that it can't blow away."

Thinking that he'd sensed something in her voice, bitterness? surely not jealousy? he'd said no more, and just waited for her to bring it back to him. She'd seemed to have forgotten about it. A few days later she'd ridden out on her horse to fetch provisions from Tintagel, and he'd searched her room. It wasn't difficult. Apart from her bed, the room contained only a blanket box, and a large chest of drawers that he'd brought back from a farm sale. At the back of the top drawer, placed neatly underneath a clean white shirt and some stockings, he found Charlotte's bonnet cap. If she'd wanted to have something that belonged to her sister, why hadn't she just asked him? He smiled. He knew where it was.

One morning at the end of the summer, as Charlotte was preparing food for the midday meal, Will knocked on the kitchen window, attracting her attention. He was pointing up towards the lane that led away from the main entrance into the farm.

"We've got a visitor! Woman with a pony and trap!"

Charlotte quickly dried her hands on her apron and hurried to the door. Their visitor, a smartly dressed young woman, stopped the pony outside the gate; climbed down from her little seat and pulled a large box from inside the trap.

"Delivery for Miss Dymond," she said, as she struggled with the gate. "Miss Charlotte Dymond Lower Penhale Farm."

"That's me, but I haven't ordered anything. There must be a mistake. Do you know who sent it?"

"No mistake miss. Nothing to pay neither. I was asked to pick it up from the dressmakers, in Camelford. I know nothing more than that." Smiling, she handed the box over to Charlotte. "One more delivery," she said as she left; "to Mrs Chapman up at Trevivian, and then I'm off home for my dinner."

As Charlotte carried the box to the table, Phillipa Peter came down from upstairs. "Who was that at the door?" she asked, her eyes on the box.

"A delivery for me mistress, but I haven't ordered anything."

"Well open it up girl. I expect there'll be a note inside." But there was not note. The box contained an exquisite primrose yellow gown, ribboned and beaded and trimmed very narrowly in a pale green. Charlotte held it up in front of her, unable to believe her eyes.

"Oh mistress, isn't it beautiful? Surely there's been some mistake."

"Well if what you say is true Charlotte, and you have no idea who sent you this gown, then it's my guess you have an admirer girl; and one with a bit of money if I'm not mistaken!"

When Matthew came in for his dinner he suggested, much to Charlotte's dismay; that the dressmakers may have mixed up their deliveries.

"Maybe the gown should have been sent to Tamson Chapman, and she has received something that was meant for you. I'll walk up there later and ask her."

"But my name is on the box," she protested. "Miss Charlotte Dymond, Lower Penhale farm. It has to be my gown." And this was confirmed later in the day. Tamson Chapman had ordered and received a blue bonnet from the dressmakers in Camelford.

Early December 1843

It was a bright, moonlit evening in early December. The air was cold, almost freezing, but Matthew had decided that it would be as good a night as any to walk up to Halworthy to see Nell and her mother. He could have a drink and something to eat in the inn afterwards, maybe a warming glass of brandy and a meat pie, before he started out on the walk back to the farm. The bag which he'd strapped to his back was heavy, crammed to the brim with the little delicate woodcarvings that he planned to give to Nell. Hopefully, she'd be able to sell them before Christmas and earn a little money. She needed the money far more than he did, and so he thought, that, because it was Christmas time, he would let her keep every penny that she made from them for herself.

The sky had clouded over by the time he reached the inn and he doubted that she would still be there, sitting in the yard with her mother. When the weather was bad, William Northam sometimes let them sit inside, but Matthew couldn't see them in the bar, and so he went through and out of the small door at the back of the building, to a large stone cobbled area, where a few hardy customers sat supping their drinks. The yard was lit only by a few lanterns which had been placed on the tables, and in the short time that it had taken Matthew to walk from the front to the back of the inn, large flakes of snow had started to fall. Nell was sitting at a table, smiling up at a bullish looking man who was picking over the bits of jewellery laid out in front of her. For a moment Matthew thought that he was going to slip a little necklace up into the sleeve of his coat, but he seemed to suddenly have a change of heart, and, placing it back on the table, he wandered away.

"I think he was going to steal something from you then. But he seemed to think better of it."

"Matthew!" Nell squealed as he sat down on the bench beside her. She turned to give him an impulsive little hug. "I wasn't expecting you tonight, it's so cold!"

"You should be inside on a night like this," he told her. "Is your mother here?"

"She went inside to warm up. We do that sometimes on nights like these. One of us watches the table, and one goes inside for a while. But now it's raining Matthew, and mother will want to pack everything up and go straight home!"

"It's snowing Nell," he touched her cheek, sad that she couldn't see the white flakes that were falling thick and fast now, all around them, glistening as they fell through the light from the lamp. She looks like a little angel he thought, with the snow clinging to her fair hair and her face, now turned up towards the sky. She was seventeen, much older than he'd thought when they first met. She was so small, so dainty that he'd thought her just a child.

"I've brought you some more of the wood carvings." He had taken his bag and laid it on the table in front of her. "You don't seem to have any of them left."

"People like them," she said. "Mother has some money for you. Maybe you should go inside and find her and then make your way back. If the snow settles it will make walking more difficult."

"I don't need to look for her," he said. "I want you to keep the money to help buy extra food for Christmas or wood for the fire. Whatever you need. And any money you can make from these carvings; keep all of that as well."

"Oh Matthew, I do love you so." Tears were slowly rolling down her face as she threw her arms around his neck.
"Nell! Whatever are you doing girl? You'll have people talking. Matthew's spoken for; you know that!"
"Oh mother, here you are. Matthew said we must keep the money we've made from his wood carvings, to help us buy food and keep warm over Christmas."
"Well that's kind of you Matthew, but we already keep half of the money, and you're saving to set up on your own and to marry your girl one day."
"If it weren't for Nell and yourself Mrs Ternouth, it's likely that I wouldn't be able to sell them at all."

Nell's mother was sorting through Matthew's bag, taking out the polished wooden animals and packing them away in her own bag.
"These are new," she said, pulling out a squirrel and a fox from amongst the birds, rabbits and horses. "Tis a wonder you've got the time to make all of these, son, with your girl out keeping you company in the woodshed while you're workin' on 'em."

Matthew was so shocked by her words that he didn't answer her at first. How would Nell's mother know his business? He certainly hadn't told them that. He liked the woman, but she was nothing like her daughter, and could be far too loud and outspoken at times.
"How do you know that about Charlotte?" he asked, the warmth drained from his voice.

"Oh I'm sorry son. Tis common knowledge what goes on at Penhale 'round these parts." Matthew was looking confused now, so she carried on. "John Westlake drinks in 'ere night times on his way home from his marshes, and when he's in drink he talks a lot about your Charlotte. Too much if you ask me. I don't think 'is wife would be too pleased if she could hear 'im carrying on! I didn't mean to upset you Matthew. I hope you've not taken offence to it."

She didn't want to fall out with Matthew Weeks. He'd been a good friend and helped them earn extra money with those wood carvings. But most of all she thought him a good catch for her Nell. He had more money than most and he'd told them he didn't want to be a servant for the rest of his life. He was caring too, and already seemed fond of her daughter. Nell certainly loved him. If it wasn't for that Charlotte Dymond she reckoned she could persuade him into marrying Nell, and then her worries for the girl would be over. After all, there weren't too many women who would chase after Matthew; not with that limp of his.

"I'm not offended Mrs Ternouth." Matthew was sounding more like himself again. "In fact I'd like you to tell me if you hear any more of what John Westlake is saying about Charlotte, or about me for that matter. Will you do that?"

Matthew's journey home wasn't easy. The snow was settling fast and was deep in places. He was cold, his ankle was aching and his mind was in turmoil. John Westlake had been talking about him, and it seemed, about everything that went on at Penhale Farm. But that wasn't what was upsetting him. Nell's mother had said that when John was in drink he was always talking about Charlotte, and that she didn't think Mary would be too happy if she could hear him. He was tired of it. He'd been noticing, more and more lately, that the men were always watching Charlotte. Tom Prout, and his brother John, William Hocken, and even John Chapman, who had a really pretty woman of his own. Old Charles Parsons had been eyeing her up and down a couple of days before. He called at the farm trying to sell them things from the box of bits and pieces that he carried around with him. He sold knives, razors, braces and small tools, as well as neck scarves and stockings and garters for the ladies. That was why Charlotte had come out to take a look, and he had to watch the old man, who had to be in his eighties, sidling up against her, making saucy remarks. She even seemed to enjoy it and had bought a new neck scarf from him! Oh, she could be shy around people that she didn't know, but she certainly like attention from those that she did know; especially when that attention came from the men. Maybe he should have a word with her. Tell her how he felt. But she would say that he was being silly, that they were just being friendly and that he should take no notice. *"Who am I keeping company with Matthew Weeks?"* she would say. *"You, not any of them, and they know that, so take no notice."* It was eating away at him though, and he didn't know if he could just *"take no notice"* not for the rest of his life. For that was what it would be like if he married Charlotte, having to take no notice for the rest of his life. But what could he do about it? The men that he was so bothered about were mostly his friends, except for Tom Prout, but they all probably wondered why Charlotte was keeping company with him. He'd been marked by the smallpox, and left with a limp. More recently, he'd had the worry that he might collapse without warning; not to mention the nose bleeds he'd been having, ever since that temperance meeting. What he really needed was a wife he wouldn't have to worry about; someone like his little Nell. Nell. He was fond of her and he didn't doubt that she would make someone a good wife. But not him, not while Charlotte was in his life, for sadly it was Charlotte that he loved.

Rosebenault Farm - Christmas Eve 1843

"Tom. You still awake?"

"Mmm. Why?"

"You int'rested in Charlotte?"

"Pippy's Charlotte?" asked Tom, reluctant to answer the question.

"Yea. I was talking with her today. I called in at the farmhouse to see if they needed any help. She's grown into a real pretty maid Tom!"

"So what were you talkin' about?"

"You mostly. She talked on and on about you. But Tom, I think she's keen on me."

Tom groaned into his pillow.

"Forget her John. She's walkin' out with Weeks. She's just a bit flighty that's all. She's the same with me."

"Yea, but Tom, why is she with Weeks? I mean ……..Weeks?"

"Well they've always been close John, and I hear he's got a bit of money now. Left it when his grandfather died."

"Well I've got a bit of money!"

Tom sat up. This was news to him.

"You John! Where'd you get money?"

"Bin' saving it up."

"Well I always thought you was a bit of a miser. Never buying me a drink! What you savin' for?"

"Well it was to buy a bit of land one day. Make something of meself."

"And now? What's it for now?"

"Well, still for the land. But I thought I might wed Charlotte when the times right. If she'll 'ave me."

Tom groaned again.

"Forget her John. She'll only bring you trouble. Find a maid who really likes you."

"What about you Tom? I thought you took a shine to Rebecca Jewell a while back. So what 'appened with that?"

"Mmm. Becky's a nice girl but not for me. She's too quiet and shy. I like a bit more of a challenge."

"Like Charlotte?"

"Mmm" and then "No John! Not like Charlotte! I just told you what I think about Charlotte.

John was laughing now and turned quickly onto his side to face the wall. He had his answer.

"Sooner we get to sleep, sooner the day'll come around."

Lower Penhale Farm – that same Christmas Eve.

It was late in the day on Christmas Eve that Rebecca Lanxon arrived at Lower Penhale Farm. She was the daughter of Mrs Peter's brother and had been born, eighteen years earlier in the parish of St Breward. Recently, however, she had married a wealthy farmer from Blisland, George Lanxon, who was twelve years her senior, and now she was expecting his child. Hearing that George was to be away on business over Christmas and into the New Year, Phillipa had invited her niece to stay over at the farm until his return. Rebecca was no stranger to Penhale as she'd often stayed before, especially at Christmas time and during the harvests.

Lower Penhale Farm – Christmas Day 1843

Phillipa Peter and Charlotte were hard at work, peeling vegetables for the Christmas meal. Soon the food would be stewing in the cauldrons, the beef roasting on the turning spit above the fire. Bread and sweetmeats, prepared the day before, had been stored away in the larder off the kitchen. There would be enough to share with anyone who came along later to join in the celebrations and to warm themselves beside the yule log as it burned in the large hearth. In the evening there would be carol singing and dancing in the barn. Family, friends, neighbours and everyone who had helped with the work on the farm during the year had been invited along. At Christmas time all were welcomed.

Mary and John Westlake and John's mother Sarah arrived early as usual with Phillipa's three young grandchildren, Eliza, Richard and Rebecca, who were all noisy and excited. When Digory and Mary Prout turned up, together with Tom and John, it was clear that the brothers had already been at the drink and as they were acting far more stupidly than the children, Phillipa turned all of the men outside, to carry on with their antics in the barn or in the yard.
She didn't care where they went, as long as they were out of her kitchen.

The day went much as every other Christmas day at Lower Penhale farm. A good time was being had by them all, but underneath the merriment, Phillipa watched as trouble stewed and began to bubble to the surface, much like the food in the cauldron over her fireplace. She watched as they all sat together around the long table to enjoy their meal, family and servants alike. Charlotte was quiet and keeping her head down. She'd been like that for months now, whenever Tom turned up at the farm. Her nephew John had seated himself next to Charlotte and was trying to draw the girl out of herself, but Tom was watching him, his neck getting redder and redder, and Phillipa suspected that this wasn't caused solely by her Christmas wine.

With dinner over, the table cleared and everything washed up and put away, Charlotte had walked over to the window seat, made herself comfortable and beckoned to Matthew, patting the empty seat beside her, inviting him to join her. But before he could make a move, Tom was there, sitting down in the empty space, turning himself around to face Charlotte with his legs drawn up and his feet resting on the window ledge in front of him. And instead of the girl getting up and moving away to join Matthew, as Phillipa had expected, she'd turned towards Tom and swung her own legs up onto the window ledge so that they sat facing each other, looking for all the world like a pair of ill-assorted bookends. And then they'd started laughing, as if something had suddenly struck them both as being very funny. So, whatever their problem had been, it seemed it was over. But Phillipa sensed a new problem. Matthew had been watching them from his seat at the table and was now up and storming through the kitchen towards the door. Sarah Westlake, who had also been watching the little scene in the window seat, stepped back in astonishment as Matthew barged his way through between her and her son John. As the door slammed shut behind Matthew, all eyes seemed to turn upon Charlotte and Tom, who were both scrambling to their feet.

"I'll go after him," Charlotte was saying as she gathered up the skirt of her best dress, ready to follow Matthew out into the yard.

"Don't fret about him maid!" John Peter called out to her. "He's likely eaten too much of mother's figgy pudding." And he roared with laughter, slapping his own leg in merriment before turning back towards Digory Prout to continue their conversation.

Tom watched Charlotte as she quietly left the kitchen and went out into the porch. He sat back down in the window seat to observe her progress as she searched around the yard. She looked in both sides of the old shed and then carefully approached the piggery, hoisting her skirts up high so as not to dirty her dress as she leaned in over the little half door. No luck there it seemed for she crossed the yard again, making for the barn, and disappeared from view. She didn't some back. Tom waited impatiently, wanting to get up and go outside to join her, but knowing at the same time that it would only cause more trouble. He saw Will and Isaac Cory walking towards the house, and watched as John Peter pounced on them both as soon as they entered the kitchen, supplying them with drinks and asking if they'd seen anything of Matthew on their way to the farm, as he'd left the kitchen earlier in a rage over some goings on between Charlotte and Tom. Will looked across at him and nodded but made his way over to sit with Rebecca Lanxon. They were about the same age, Will and Rebecca, and had known each other from small children. She looked pleased to see him and they were soon engaged in a lively conversation. Tom watched them for a while, wishing that someone would look that pleased to see him. Where was his brother John? This was partly John's fault for sitting

159

beside Charlotte like that; letting her drink all that wine. She would never have behaved like that with him in front of Matthew if it wasn't for the wine. But he couldn't blame John. His brother had declared his own interest in Charlotte only the night before, as well as giving him the chance to speak out if he felt anything himself for the girl. And he'd denied those feelings. Denied the love he'd held for her ever since that day in the barn when he'd scolded her for flirting with him. He was a fool. She'd been sixteen then, and already promised to Weeks. She was seventeen now though, and he was sure that she felt something for him in return. Why else would she have been acting so strangely since the day of that teetotal festival out on the moor? He knew he'd embarrassed her and that she'd been angry with him, but surely not so angry that she would just shut him out in the way that she had, for months on end. She'd barely spoken to him in all that time, and had always seemed to find a reason to leave a room whenever he had entered it. She wasn't comfortable with the way that she was treating him either. He could tell that. And there had been times; times when she couldn't get away from him, that he'd caught her watching him, and his eyes had been able to hold hers for a few moments before she'd looked away again. But he hadn't ever been able to read anything in them. Maybe now things would be better between them, and he would be able to tell her how he felt, before she married Weeks and was lost to him for ever. He looked back at Will and Rebecca again. They were talking about him now, he was sure of it, Rebecca kept glancing over in his direction. And then she held out her hand for Will to help her to her feet, and together they walked over to where both of his aunts were sitting with his mother.

"Will and I are going outside to speak with Charlotte," she said. "We shall be right back if all is well. It's very cold out there today."

Tom got to his feet. "I'll go with them," he called over to his Phillipa Peter. "Maybe talk to Matthew." But she shook her head and motioned for him not to follow them. He sank back down in the seat again. She was right. There was nothing that he could do today that would help matters.

"Any room on here for me?" His brother John was squeezing in beside him, handing him a beer. "You found your challenge then Tom boy," he said quietly.

"It would seem so John," Tom replied, raising his glass. "It would certainly seem so."

Outside Rebecca pulled her shawl tightly around herself against the cold. "Where shall we look first then Will, the barn or the stable?"

"Oh the barn," he said. "And quickly. You shouldn't be out too long in this weather with a baby on the way."

They saw Charlotte straight away, as soon as Will pulled the barn door open and the light streamed in. She was sitting on the edge of a small stack of hay, with one of the little terrier dogs on her lap.

"Have you seen Matthew?" Will asked as she looked up at them.

She shook her head, her eyes bright with tears. "I'll see if I can find him." Will left them, closing the door behind him and Rebecca picked up an old milking stool and sat down on it beside Charlotte.

"Which one is this then?" she asked, stroking the little dog. Is it Charlie?"

"No, it's Issy, his mother." Issy's tail wagged at the mention of her name.

"Any pups this winter?" Rebecca was looking hopefully around the apparently empty barn.

"Not one, and none in the summer either. I miss them. I think Issy may be too old now to have any more pups." And as Charlotte spoke, tears began to stream down her face.

"Dear girl," Rebecca reached out for Charlotte's hand. "Why are you so unhappy? You've always been so close to Matthew. Surely this is just a silly tiff and will be over as soon as he returns. I don't blame him though for walking out, for it's no secret that he's never liked Thomas, and there you were, sitting in the window seat with him and laughing together as if it were the two of you that are keeping company, instead of you and Matthew."

"I love him Rebecca. I love Thomas."

"Charlotte, this is the wine talking! You had at least four glasses at dinner. I was watching you. It will all look quite different in the morning, you'll see."

"Another day will make no difference Rebecca. It's been seven months now. Seven months since the teetotal festival at Roughtor when he picked me up, right in front of Matthew, and demanded a kiss from me. He'd won some ridiculous wrestling match and we were in the middle of a crowd of jeering ruffians. It was horrid Rebecca. But ………."

"You didn't kiss him Charlotte!"

"Of course not. But I wanted to. And I still want to. And I've tried so hard not to love him."

"Does he know Charlotte? Does Thomas know how you feel about him?"

"No. He couldn't possibly. I've been perfectly horrible to him ever since."

"Then he probably does know. And what of Matthew? Have you told him anything of this?"

"Matthew's always working. If he's not working on the farm, he's across the yard in his carpentry shed, making things that he can sell, so that one day he'll have enough money to set up on his own as a carpenter, and marry me. How can I tell him?"

"Well this can't continue Charlotte. Something must be done about it. But maybe not today. Come back inside with me. We'll make ourselves a brew of tea and sit by the fire. I'm chilled to the bone."

"There's a storm on the way." Phillipa was saying, as the girls came back into the farmhouse. She was standing in the open doorway at the back of the kitchen, looking up at the sky above the mowhay. "I pray Matthew's not out there in the cold. He had no coat with him."

"Matthew will be over with the Chapmans, or up with the Haynes on their farm. The man's not an idiot." John Peter was sprawled out on the settle talking to Isaac Cory, who had pulled over the chair at the bottom of the stairs to sit beside him. "I pray," John said, pulling a face at Isaac. "I pray that he walks back in before the evening's done, or she'll have us all out with lanterns searching for him in the fields."

A flash of lightning in the open doorway startled them all, and the distant rumble of thunder brought Maria Cory to her feet to pull all the curtains across the windows. "If there's one thing I don't like it's a thunder storm," she said, sitting back down again, well away from the windows. The wind was getting up and hail stones began to beat in through the open door. Phillipa quite liked a storm, but she closed the door quickly for the sake of her guests.

"It'll be carol singing in the barn tonight then," she declared, shaking the little icy stones from her hair. "No one's going to want to stand outside in this."

"I shouldn't think there'll be many of us tonight," remarked John Peter. "No one else is going to turn up in weather like this mother."

The hail turned to rain and the sound of the thunder came closer and closer as the storm raged outside, until, at around six o'clock, a flash of lightning lit up the kitchen through the porch way and Tom pulled back the curtains behind the window ledge to look outside. "Someone's out there," he said. There's a horse and cart coming down the lane. It looks like John Chapman and Will, and Matthew's with them."
"Well thank the Lord for that." John Peter heaved himself out of his comfortable seat. "Let's get them inside."

But the little party arriving from the direction of Trevivian that night were a very sorry sight to behold as they came in from the storm. All soaked to the skin, Will and John were supporting Matthew between them.
"It's not looking good for him Mrs Peter." The two Johns laid Matthew down on the settle. "Will found him in the lane close to my house. He must have tripped, because his head's hit a stone and he was out cold, dead to the world. His breathing's bad too. We took him back to the house and cleaned his head up a bit, and he came around for a while, but he keeps slipping away again. We thought he would be best off here, going to his own bed, but I think he'll need the doctor in the morning."

Phillipa Peter took charge. "Well, it's a mercy you found him Will. I think it's best you sleep back at home for a few nights, just until Matthew's more like himself again. Do you think you could help the master get Matthew up the stairs and put some dry clothes on him? I'll be up as soon as he's dried off and you've got him into his bed. John will ride over to Camelford in the morning to fetch the doctor. Charlotte! Stop wailing girl and bring us all something to eat. Mary will help you. There'll be no carol singing or dancing tonight."

"I'm sorry to be the bearer of bad news Mrs Peter, but I'm afraid that your young servant Matthew's condition is quite grave."
"Oh Doctor Bennett. Whatever is wrong with him?"
Phillipa Peter ushered the doctor over from the bottom of the stairs to sit at her kitchen table. She motioned to her niece, and to Charlotte, to come and join them.
"Is it the congestion? Matthew is in his seventh year of service with us on the farm and we think very highly of him. Charlotte here has been keeping company with him for more than a year now, and my niece will be staying with us for a while longer. He will be well looked after."

"I am sure dear lady, I am sure, but it isn't the congestion that is worrying me, or indeed the head wound. It is his heart. Matthew has been telling me that he didn't trip over, as you had all supposed, before falling and hitting his head, but that in fact he passed out in the lane, and that this has happened to him on several occasions in the past. In light of this, I have examined him and found that his heart beats in a most irregular way. Most irregular. This will, I fear, cause him to pass out from time to time without warning."

"But he has said nothing of this to me. How long has this been going on? Charlotte! Has Matthew told you anything of this?"

The girl's face was drained of colour. "I know that he fainted on Mrs Mudge's door step when he thought that Thomasine and I had the smallpox. And he did say that the same thing happened to him once before that, on his way to his mother's house."

"And did you not think that I would need to know this? Does Matthew think me so uncaring that he would not tell me such a thing?"

"Oh no mistress. Matthew is always saying how good you are to us and how fortunate we are to have such a kind mistress, and the master too. He is very happy here. We are both very happy here."

But Phillipa Peter was still looking very distressed. "What of his work on the farm doctor? It can be a very hard life at times as you must know, and he is often working alone out in the fields."

"It is possible that being a farm labourer is not the best work for Matthew. Very possible dear lady, but I presume that the young man has little choice in the matter."

"But Matthew has skills in the carpentry trade and in the blacksmith trade, doesn't he aunt? I understand that he wishes to set up on his own as a carpenter one day." Rebecca spoke out unexpectedly and immediately regretted her words.

"More secrets. I know nothing of him setting up on his own. I shall have words with him when he is well enough, and with you Charlotte as soon as Doctor Bennett has left us. But for now doctor, what must we do to help our patient? I sat beside him all through last night, and his chest was so tight that he had great difficulty with his breathing."

Early March 1844

It was the second week of March before Matthew felt well enough to walk up to Halworthy again. His mistress had been far from happy about his going, but she had agreed to let him have the Saturday as his day off so that he might see Nell and her mother, since the inn would be closed on the Sunday.

"I really don't know why you should want to see them Matthew," she had said as he prepared to leave the farmhouse, dressed very smartly as usual. "You have no new carvings for them. You haven't been out in the woodshed once since your illness. But it is none of my business what you do on your days off. I know that. I am your employer, not your mother. Make no mistake though Matthew, I intend to see that no harm comes to you while you are working for me on the farm. Come Lady Day I shall be taking on another servant to do some of the heavier jobs, and to work in the fields that are the farthest away from the house. If you wish to go climbing up to the top of Roughtor or walking to visit your mother on a Sunday, then I cannot stop you." She had laughed then and sent him on his way.

It was true that he had nothing to take for Nell and her mother. He hadn't been well enough to work out in his shed in the cold winter weather, and had preferred to stay in the warmth of the farmhouse kitchen, spending his time with Charlotte. As long ago as the autumn, she had seemed to tire of spending her evenings with him in the woodshed, and on Sundays, when they would normally have spent their time together walking on the moor, or in the lanes, she had chosen rather to visit with the Chapmans, or with the Haynes family at Tremail.

She seemed happy to be with him again now though, since his illness. In the evenings they sat side by side on the settle, or if John Peter was at home, in the window seat, talking and laughing as if nothing had ever come between them. They had never been lovers as Charlotte's mind was set on waiting until they were married. She had made it clear, as far back as when they had first started keeping company that she did not want to be like her mother, and her grandmother before that, having babies without being wed to their fathers. He understood that, respected her for it, but it was hard at times. Even his sister Janey was married now and living in Plymouth with her husband, and as a result, his mother had an empty bedroom in her house at Larrick. He planned to visit her soon and had thought that he might ask her if he could go back home to live. He would marry Charlotte and take her there as his wife; ask his uncle if he could work for him again; improve his skills as a carpenter. His mother would probably be glad of the money it would bring into the house, glad to have their company. He hadn't said anything of his plan to anyone, not even to Charlotte, and before he could do that he would have to walk the eleven miles to his mother's house and talk with her and with his uncle, to see if they would agree to help him.

As Matthew reached Halworthy Inn that day he took note of the time on his pocket watch. It was almost one o'clock. He was pleased with himself. He had walked slowly, not wanting to pass out in the road, although he knew that by choosing to walk in daylight, he would have been found without much time passing by. He had completed his journey of around three miles in less than two hours and would have been at his destination even earlier if he hadn't stopped to pass the time of day with two old acquaintances. William Northam was behind the bar, and so Matthew went to buy himself a drink and stayed talking for a while before looking around for Nell and her mother. They were sitting in the corner nearest to the fire, and Mrs Ternouth leaned across to whisper in her daughter's ear before getting to her feet to greet him as he crossed the room to join them.

"So you are well again. You don't know what a relief it is to see you son."

Matthew took her outstretched hands, and then reached down to take Nell's hand in his before sitting down beside her. The girl didn't speak but her face shone with happiness.

"I thought that you would hear of my illness through John Westlake."

Mrs Ternouth nodded and looked away from him, down at the table.

"I haven't brought you any carvings I'm afraid. It's been too cold for me to work outside in the evenings."

"We weren't expecting any, son, though we have sold all of those that you brought here in December. We ate well over Christmas, and all because of your generosity." She was still looking down at the table. "Matthew, you asked me to tell you if I knew anymore of what John Westlake has been saying about you, or indeed about Charlotte." She paused, looking up at him again. He nodded slowly.

"Go on Mrs Ternouth."

"Well he's been saying Matthew, that Charlotte prefers another. A nephew of Mrs Peter by the name of Thomas Prout."

Nell was squeezing one of his hands tightly. "And I was hoping Matthew," she said, suddenly finding her voice, "that if you are no longer with Charlotte, you

might consider keeping company with me. This year is leap year, and so a girl may ask a young man ......"
He had left them. Pulling his hand away from hers, he had struggled to his feet and left them.

"Have we lost him Mother?" Nell spoke softly, her face stricken with grief. "Have we lost Matthew?"
"I fear so child," Mrs Ternouth replied. "I do fear so."

At around three o'clock that same Saturday afternoon, Charlotte came out of the farmhouse with scraps of food for the hens. As 'her girls' scurried towards her from all corners of the yard, she thought she heard something drop to the floor inside the barn. Quickly scattering the food around to the birds, she ran over and entered the barn through the open door. A pitch fork lay in the middle of the floor, and so she looked around to see what had caused it to fall. The men would never leave anything like that lying around; it was too dangerous.

"Charlotte." His voice made her jump. Tom was standing in the shadows beside the door. In her haste she had rushed straight past him.
"I heard something fall." She looked around to see if Will or John Peter were there with him.
"I dropped the pitch fork. I knew it would bring you into the barn."
She was glad that he didn't know how disturbed she felt, finding herself alone with him.

"I must go Tom, I have work to do."
"Nothing that can't wait. Not at this time of day."

She moved to pass by him and go to the door, but Tom held out his arm, blocking her way. Gently he turned her around and lifted her face to look into his.

"Charlotte," he said again as he kissed her, his throat aching somewhere deep inside as she kissed him back.

"Lucky Matthew," he said, his voice sounding strange to his own ears. "Leave him Charlotte. You want me. I know you do. Marry me. We'll find a way through all of this."

But she pulled away from him and fled out of the barn, towards the house.

"Damn Weeks!" He cursed as he smashed his hand on the door. "That girl should be mine!"

Misfortune struck again for Matthew as he returned to the farm at that exact moment, and saw Charlotte running blindly passed him as Tom swore and hit the barn door.

"What have you done Tom Prout?" he demanded. "What have you done to Charlotte?"

"If you must know I asked her to marry me!" Tom glared at him and slammed the barn door back against the stone wall. "She belongs with me Weeks, but you're too stupid to see it."

"And what was her answer?" Matthew lunged towards Tom, pulling him out into the yard and Tom's hand shot out, grabbing Matthew by his shirt collar and ripping it.

"She ran from me this time. You saw her. But I will ask her again, and again, until she says yes to me!"

Phillipa Peter was watching from the porch way. She had come outside to see what was wrong after Charlotte had burst into her kitchen, sobbing and running straight up over the stairs. To her relief, John appeared from around the side wall of the stable and, without a word, took hold of both men by their shoulders and forced them apart. For a moment she thought John might crack their heads together, but Tom pushed his arm away and stepped back, holding up both of his hands.

"I wasn't going to hit him John," he said. "Don't worry, I'm going."

He turned and walked away, in the direction of Rosebenault.

Back in the kitchen again, Matthew stood looking up at the top of the stairs. "Has she gone up to her room?" he asked. His mistress nodded. "I'll go up and speak with her," he said, but Phillipa knew that he was waiting for her permission. She nodded again and watched as he slowly climbed up and out of sight. He looks broken, she thought. All the anger had gone from him in a moment, and he looked broken and defeated.

Her door was open and she was sitting quietly on her bed, just looking out of the window towards the mowhay.

"What has happened to us?" He sat down beside her. "I came straight back from Halworthy because I heard at the inn that you preferred Tom to me. And when I get here, the man tells me that he has asked you to marry him and that I am too stupid to see that you want him. Is it true Charlotte? Do you want to be with Tom?"

"I....I....," she was stuttering, her normally pale face flushed. "Who was speaking about me at the inn?"

"Well there's my answer. I have lost you." He buried his face in his hands but she clutched at his arm.

"I love you Matthew," she said, "I always will, but I can't stop thinking about Tom. That's the truth of it, and now you know. What will you do?"

He was losing her and he knew it, but he took his hands from his face and put his arm around her. She dropped her head on his shoulder and they sat together like this for a while until he said, "I have plans Charlotte and I will see them through, whether you are beside me or not. So we'll say nothing of this downstairs, until Tom comes back and then you must decide." He kissed her then, holding her face in his hands.

"Whatever happens," he said, "I'll always love you Charlotte Dymond."

On the following Monday Phillipa Peter was sorting through the clothes that were to be washed that day. The white shirt that Matthew had worn up to Halworthy two days before was torn on the shoulder and the collar button was hanging by a thread.

"Charlotte," she said, "This shirt of Matthew's will have to be mended before it is washed, to save it from ripping even further. I don't know what Matthew spoke to you about on Saturday when he came up to your room, and I don't wish to, but I do know that this shirt is ripped as a result of whatever went on in the barn between you and my nephew, and that those two men almost came to blows over it. If it weren't for John stepping in when he did, well ...... I don't want to think about what would have happened, I really don't. I turned a blind eye to your goings on at Christmas for Matthew's sake, but now it seems that I was mistaken in that, and so I'm warning you now Charlotte, that if I see any more enmity between those two men because of you, I shall have to let you go. I cannot ask Matthew to leave, for he has done nothing wrong. If he wishes to go one day for his own reasons then that will be different. Thomas of course is my nephew and will always be welcomed here, and so I have no choice in this matter young woman. I hope that you understand me."

Charlotte did understand her mistress, but she didn't know what she was going to do about it. Tom had gone away, presumably back to his place of service at Helset, several miles away in the parish of Lesnewth. She did not know when he would return; only that now she wanted to be with him more than ever she had before. Matthew was allowing her to choose between them. His love for her was so true, that if it weren't for Tom, she knew she would be happy spending her life with him. If only there was someone to turn to. She hadn't heard from her mother in years, or indeed from James Medland, the man who thought he was her father. Her mistress was fond of her, she knew that, but it had been made very clear that the men, and family loyalty came first. Rebecca Lanxon would help her if she could, but she was living miles away, and now had a new-born to look after. They had spent some time talking together after Christmas; through all of those days when Matthew had been so ill, and they had been helping to care for him. Rebecca had told her then that she thought she should make a new life for herself, away from the farm. She had spent, she'd told her, too many years shut away on the edge of the moor. *"Come to Blisland with me,"* she had said. *"You don't have to work on our farm. You could live with us and find employment nearby. There is a schoolhouse being built in the village. It will be ready soon. You can read and write Charlotte, and your mother was a schoolmistress. I am quite sure that you would be as capable of teaching the children as anyone. Miss Charlotte Dymond, the schoolmistress at Blisland village!"* It had sounded exciting at the time, but Rebecca had gone back to her husband, and she had heard nothing more from her, except of course for the news of the baby.

At the end of the week Phillipa Peter declared that she intended to travel into Bodmin to the Saturday market and she asked Charlotte to go with her. Nothing more had been said about the previous Saturday so Charlotte agreed straight away, asking if she might be allowed to visit with Emily Mudge, while she was in town. But her hopes were quickly dashed.

"Mrs Mudge is away Charlotte," John Peter said. "Staying with her in-laws at Port Isaac for a while. I saw Doctor Jenkins only last week and he was saying how difficult he was finding it, with her not being there."

Saturday 16th March, 1844. - Bodmin

Ben Kircher finished his ale and prepared to leave the Royal Hotel. He had business with the saddler on the folly, but as he walked out into the bustle of Fore Street, he saw her, directly across the street from him, in the doorway of the dressmakers shop. She was looking around, looking for someone he thought, but then her eyes lit on him and stayed fixed, staring across at him as if in sudden shock. He crossed the street, smiling at her. "Charlotte?"

She nodded. "Ben?" she said quietly. "Ben Kircher?"

"So you recognise me now then? You didn't seem to know me the last time you set eyes on me. Looked right at me you did Charlotte, and then just fell asleep on that kind looking crippled boy's shoulder."

"I still do," she said, "fall asleep on his shoulder that is. We're still good friends."

Somewhere inside she was horrified at herself. Talking to him like this in the street. She didn't really know him at all, but somehow it was as if seven years had just rolled away and they were talking together outside the Trevalga Inn, before he had gone off to find her mother. He was looking quite different, Charlotte thought, not dressed like a travelling man now, but rather more like the other men in the market town that day. His dark hair was streaked with grey, and his handsome face quite weather beaten, but she would have known that face anywhere. She used to draw it, when she was a child, on any bit of paper she could find, then scribble over the top before her mother saw it. She'd drawn it so many times that in the end she didn't need to do it anymore. She could clearly recall that face whenever she thought about him. It was clearer to her now, she realised, than her own mother's face.

"I am your father Charlotte," he said. "I don't know what your mother told you about me, but if you could only see my daughter Unity then you would believe me. She's around here somewhere but I can't see her now."

He was looking away from her, looking around for his daughter, but Charlotte caught hold of his arm.

"I do believe you," she said, bringing his attention straight back to her. "I don't know why, but I do believe you. I heard what you said to my mother that day at Trevalga. I heard more than I ever let on, even to her, and I always felt that you were telling the truth. She lied to me that day."

"We all lie Charlotte. You're old enough to know that now. Mostly because we think it's for the best at the time. Your mother was only trying to protect you."

"But why didn't you come back?" she asked him. "After you found me again, why didn't you ever come back?"

"I did Charlotte?" he said, placing his hand over hers on his arm. "It was three years later, but I did come back. They said you'd left the farm, moved on, and no one would tell me where you'd gone. They don't like telling strangers their business Charlotte, not the Cornish. Especially not travelling people like me."

He was looking at her closely, taking in every feature on her face. "Is he your young man then?" he asked. "The crippled boy whose shoulder you fall asleep on."

"Matthew? He is; well he was until two weeks ago that is. We're still friends but ...." Her voice faltered and now it was his turn to feel horrified as he saw her eyes begin to fill up with tears.

"What's wrong Charlotte? I didn't mean to upset you!"

"Oh no," she shook her head. "It's not your fault. It's just that everything's gone wrong ......" And her voice trailed away. She was trying so hard not to cry.

"We must talk Charlotte. Maybe I can help. But not here. Can you get away from the farm somewhere quiet where folk won't see us together, for it won't do your reputation any good, being seen out with me."

"I can only get away on Sundays," she said. "Matthew and I used to climb up to the top of Roughtor on Sundays sometimes, after chapel. But we don't now. And this weekend he's going home to see his mother, so ...."

Her voice trailed way again as she heard her mistress calling her.

"Charlotte! Where are you girl?"

Charlotte turned to see her mistress approaching.

"Roughtor it is then," he said quickly, "Tomorrow. But make it Roughtor Ford, just a little downstream from the bridge. We won't be seen there. About an hour after afternoon chapel."

She nodded and he very quickly disappeared into the crowded street.

"Who's that you were talking to Charlotte?" Mrs Peter was up at her side. "I can't leave you for a moment before you're making up to some poor man."

"He spoke to me first mistress. He said that I looked just like his daughter. That was all we spoke about."

"He's right Charlotte. I think I saw her. I thought it was you first off. She was just standing across the street over there, and when I realised she wasn't you at all, I followed her gaze and there you were, talking to that man. She was watching you. Dead spit of you she is. Maybe a bit younger. But it looks like they've both gone now, so we must away home. Did you buy yourself a new bonnet cap?"

"No mistress. I didn't much like the lace on the ones they had in the shop."

"You're far too fussy my girl. They'll make you pay more for bringing it out to the farm. You should be saving your money now Charlotte, you know that. You might be needing it soon." And she bustled off to pick up her pony and trap, which she'd left in the stables at the Royal Hotel.

Charlotte sighed and slowly began to follow her mistress, looking around as she walked, hoping for just one more glimpse of her father, or even of her half-sister. But they were nowhere to be seen.

"I'll be here tomorrow for dinner mistress," Matthew said that evening. "I don't want to walk to my mothers with it so wet underfoot." He got up from the table and went to sit on the chair by the fire. Phillipa nodded. The first two months of the year had been very wet and so far there had been little improvement in March. It had been dry that day, but now the rain had started up again outside. Charlotte was reading in the window seat but put her book down and went to sit on the settle near Matthew. Before long they were deep in conversation; seeming as friendly together as they had ever been, but they were keeping their voices so low that their mistress could hear nothing of what they had to say to one another.

"If you are not visiting with your mother tomorrow, will you walk out to Roughtor ford with me?"

"Maybe." Matthew answered her cautiously. "Why all the way out there? It will be very muddy."

"I have to meet someone; an hour after chapel in the afternoon."

"At the ford Charlotte? Why ever did you agree to that? You never go out on the moor on your own."

"That is why I am asking Matthew, but if you will not come with me, I shall have to go on my own."

Matthew grimaced. She had asked him once, never to leave her alone on the moor.

"I'll not let you do that. I'll walk with you; but who would you want to meet out there Charlotte? It makes no sense."

"I'll explain tomorrow, but you must promise not to speak of it to anyone. I know that I can trust you, but if word of this gets out it could make things very difficult for my mother."

"Your mother? Are you meeting your mother?"

"No Matthew. Not my mother. I'm meeting my father."

Sunday 17th March, 1844

He was waiting for her by the little cove in the bend of the river, just a little way from the ford; his horse tethered up nearby.

"Isn't that Matthew?" he asked, watching her companion limping away from them towards Roughtor. "I thought you mentioned him being away this weekend? Would you like him to stay here with us? I can go after him."

"No, he likes wandering about out here, but he won't go far from us today. He's not been well."

"You were here with him the last time I saw you, but you were up in the arms of another man and poor Matthew was looking very angry. It all seemed to end happily though. I saw the other man go back to the wrestling ring and you walking off with Matthew, your head on his shoulder."

"You were here that day? You saw Tom make such a show of me? But you are wrong; it didn't end happily. That *'other man'* is my mistress's nephew, Thomas Prout, and he is the reason that I was so upset when I met you in Bodmin yesterday."

She sat down on a little crop of granite stones and he sat beside her while she poured her problems out to him as if he were her oldest friend. When she had finished her story she sat looking at him, twisting the coral beads that were about her neck around in her fingers, waiting for him to say something. What could he say? He had wished, back in the summer at the teetotal festival, that he could be around to help her, and now that he had the opportunity, he didn't even know what to say! At a loss for the right words, he gently scolded her.

"You'll break those beads, turning them like that."

"Matthew gave them to me, almost two years back now, when he told me of his dream that we might marry one day. He bought them, from a little blind girl. She sells jewellery, out in the yard up at the Halworthy Inn. She told him that no two necklaces are ever fashioned the same."

"There is an unusual cut to the beads," he said laughing, "and I can tell they're strongly made!"

"Why are you here?" she asked suddenly. "In Cornwall I mean. You were here in the summer and you are still here. Where are you living?"

"I have settled here now," he said, "I have some land on the coast at Trebarwith and I'm breeding horses, raising up the foals; it's the only way that I know, but I was tired of travelling and wanted to put down roots. I have always loved the north coast of Cornwall. Your sister is with me."

And then he saw a way that he could help her. "Why don't you come and stay with us for a while. I think you need to get away from all this. Come and help us on the farm, walk on the beaches with us, ride the horses on the cliff tops. From what you have told me I'm sure that your mistress will let you leave her service."

He was offering her a way of life that she knew she would love; telling her as Rebecca Lanxon had told her, that she needed to build a new life for herself, away from Lower Penhale Farm. But what of Matthew? What of Tom? Could she bear to just walk away from them?

"What would your mother say though Charlotte?" He was looking at her anxiously. "She didn't want to know me when we met at Trevalga that day."

"She doesn't want to know me either," Charlotte said bitterly. "I don't have to worry about what she would say. She hasn't spoken to me in almost seven years."
"But why is that? You seemed so close. Why did she send you away? I always wondered."

She took a deep breath and decided that if he was now to be a part of her life, then he should know. So she told him about James Medland, the well-to-do butcher who had helped to bring her up and thought that he was her father. She told him about the gypsy women who had called at their house and warned them of a butcher bringing death into their lives and cutting a young life short before it's time. He listened as she explained her fear of having James Medland move in with them, especially as she suspected that he wasn't her real father.
"My mother told an old friend that she thought the gypsy women would return one day and take me away from her," she said, now twisting the corner of her shawl between her fingers. "That's why her friend brought me out to live at Penhale Farm. He knew that they needed a maid."

"But none of that explains why she would not have you home again from time to time. What reason could she have for never visiting you, never speaking with you again?"
A little tear was trickling down over Charlotte's cheek, but he waited for her to continue.

"Before she sent me away I told her that if James Medland came to live with us, I would tell him that he wasn't my real father. I would tell him about you."

"And what would he have done then? Turned you both out onto the streets? Had you both put into a workhouse? Didn't your mother warn you of these things? She wouldn't have known where to find me. I was a travelling man; what we had together was so brief; just an afternoon of madness."

She was looking at him in astonishment, so he went on.

"I'll tell you about it one day. We were both very young Charlotte, not much older than you are now. She should have told you that I meant nothing to her; that he was the one who had cared for you, been a father to you."

"It would have made no difference to me then," she said sadly, "I didn't want him living with us. I didn't want to share my mother with him. I would have done anything to stop that happening. I believe that is the real reason why she wouldn't have me home again."

He fell silent then, shifting around uncomfortably on the crop of stones.

I have driven him away now, she thought. He hates me as my mother must have hated me. But to her surprise he suddenly moved closer to her and put his arm around her shoulder.

"God help us then daughter," he said, "for you have my mother's ways. My father died when I was young and she made my life hard, not letting anyone get close to me, even though we were travelling with family; aunts, uncles, cousins. And when I met Maggie, Unity's mother, she did all that she could to force us apart. It was only when I told her that Maggie was expecting my child that she allowed us to marry. Even then she only tolerated her, though she did love her granddaughter, and when my infant son died, shortly after his poor mother, she was broken hearted."

"You had a son then. I had a half-brother."

"Yes Charlotte, you had a brother, but he only lived for a few weeks. Unity was with me when I found him dead in his little bed, looking for all the world as though he was asleep. We had all thought him a healthy little man, but then these things happen sometimes don't they? That was a hard time for us, losing the both of them so close together. It was after her mother's death that I told her about you, but then we didn't speak of it again until we came to live at Trebarwith."

"Are you sure that Unity would want me to come to live with you, even if it is just for a while?"

"She will love you. You mustn't worry about that. She has never seemed to mind sharing me with others. Shall I go home and say that you are coming to stay with us? We will have to do things properly though Charlotte. It's one week before Lady Day now and the end of the quarter year. Mrs Peter could release you from her service then. And you should try to tell your mother something of this, whether she is interested or not. I don't want her to think that your gypsy father has stolen you away!"

"I can't decide today father. I have to talk to Matthew, and to Tom when he comes back to the farm. I am grateful to you for trying to help me but I need to think it through."

He was looking disappointed and she was glad to see Matthew walking towards them along the river bank.

"I think Matthew's tired of waiting for me," she said, standing up and putting her shawl around her shoulders. "I must go father."

"You could send for him you know," he said, "or for Tom if he's the one you want. I can always do with an extra pair of hands about the place. Do you think four weeks will be enough time for you to decide daughter? I'll come back, four weeks from today at around the same time, and if you're here to meet me you can jump on the back of my horse and come to live with us at Trebarwith for as long as you wish. But if you're not here, I'll know that you've made other plans. I'll understand, but I'll not lose you again Charlotte. Whichever way it goes, I'll tell Unity to prepare to meet her sister one day soon."

"So you're going to go off with him now are you?" Matthew was angry with her as they walked together back to Penhale farmhouse. "Going to ride away from me to live on the coast and walk on the cliff tops with your sister. Why is he putting these ideas in your head? You hardly know him."

"It's not like that Matthew," she said. "He thinks that I need to get away for a while, that's all. I haven't agreed to anything. Rebecca Lanxon said the same to me at Christmas. She thought that I should go to Blisland and live with her; find an easier position for myself; teach at the new schoolhouse or something. I don't know what to think."

"And he wants you to tell your mother! Why would she care? You haven't seen her in years. I'll have no part in that Charlotte. Don't think that I'm walking up to Tresparrett Post with you. I have no time for your mother."

They arrived back at the farmhouse too late to help their mistress with the milking. She didn't complain because Sunday was their day off. They didn't have to be back to do any of the work, though she was grateful when they were and did agree to help. It took her the best part of two hours to milk the cows on her own, and by the end of it her back would be breaking.

Saturday 23rd March, 1844

Another week had passed and still Tom had not
returned to Lower Penhale farm. Charlotte tossed and
turned in her little bed, unable to sleep. The moon
was unusually bright and seemed low in the sky, its
light shining in through her open curtains, inviting her
to go outside. Somewhere below her one of the dogs
barked, but the rest of the house was silent; everyone
was fast asleep. Quickly putting on some clothes over
her nightdress, she crept downstairs, tiptoed through
the kitchen and out into the yard, stopping only to take
an old coat of her mistress's from its hook in the porch
way, and throw it over her shoulders. As she leaned
on the old gate, looking across at the cattle shed, Issy
squeezed out around the edge of the barn door and
came over to sit at her feet, happy to have this
unexpected company. When John Prout had stopped
by, earlier in the day, she'd asked him for news of
Tom. *"Nobody's seen Tom around here as I know of,'*
he'd said, *'not for a couple of weeks anyway. He's
more than likely licking his wounds, back up at Helset.
Don't bother yourself with him Charlotte,'* he'd joked
with her, *'You can always walk out with me if you're
tired of Matthew. I'm willing and I'll wager I've got
more money than the both of them put together."*
Word had spread quickly of the argument between
Matthew and Tom. John Peter had seen to that.

*"I've got enough problems without you adding to
them,"* she'd told him. But she had wondered if he
would walk out on the moor with her in April to see
her father, if all else failed. She had a plan of her own
and that was another reason for needing to see Tom.
She wanted to tell him how she felt about him, but she
also wanted him to take a letter to her mother. His

place of work was less than two miles from Tresparrett Post. In her letter she would ask if she could return to live with them now that she had grown up and was far too old to be taken away by gypsies. She wouldn't be able to say too much in a letter, for fear that James would read it, but she could say just that she understood why her mother had sent her away, and that if she was allowed to return she would promise to give her no cause for concern. It was, in truth, all that she had ever wanted; to go home again. She had missed her mother sorely over the years. And she was sure that Tom would take her letter, knowing that if she came to Tresparrett Post, she would be living close by to him. She had decided that she didn't want to go with her father to Trebarwith. Matthew was right. She didn't really know him and she wasn't at all sure what her sister would think of it. But she would go to Roughtor Ford and tell him herself in April. She didn't want to lose him, now that she had found him again.

One of the horses was moving about restlessly in the stable. Thinking that it might be Hercules, she went to calm him.

"Would a letter to her mother be enough?"

Within minutes Hercules was saddled up and with a lantern in her hand, Charlotte was leading him out of the yard and into the field beside it. She swung herself up into the saddle and they were off. To Tresparret Post.

She hadn't been on a horse for years but he was a dream to ride. Solid and safe. The moon was still bright, lighting their way, and she had the lantern if it should cloud over. In what seemed to her like no time at all, she was close to home, riding into the hamlet where she had been born; Hercules' hooves clopping along the rough stony surface towards her mother's cottage. There was a light in a downstairs window, so she dismounted, tethered the horse to the gatepost and peered through the parted curtains, into the room that had once been their schoolroom. James was sitting in a chair, his eyes closed, his dark hair mostly turned to silver. She tapped on the glass. His eyes flew open and seeing her in the window he jumped up and came to the door.

"Charlotte! It is you, isn't it? I thought it was your mother come back! Whatever are you doing here child? It's the middle of the night. But come in, come in."

He sat her down in his comfortable chair.

"I couldn't sleep upstairs," he said, "I had this feeling that something was going to happen tonight, but I didn't expect this! Your mother's not here Charlotte. My Margaret is expecting her third any day now, and Mary's gone to help with the older ones."

He brought a chair from the table and sat down in front of her. "What's happened to bring you here like this? Have you run away? We thought the Peters were good people and that you were happy. Simon Baker said that they treat you like family, and that you have a young man there."

"I haven't run away. I'm going back tonight, but I want to ask you to let me come home. I'm not a child anymore, afraid of gypsy prophesies. They won't want to take me away now, and I am sorry for thinking that you would have hurt me. I know that there was no truth in it. I've been happy on the farm; Simon Baker was right; but now I just want to come home."

"Well if it was up to me Charlotte; but your mother always said that you were safer on the farm. I tried child. When you were younger, I tried to make her change her mind, but she was afraid for you and as time went by she wouldn't even talk to me about it."

"Why did she never come to see me, or write to me? I haven't even had a letter from her in more than six years."

"She only said that if she saw you again she would want you back living with us, and as that couldn't be, she couldn't see you. Nothing more. As to letters; I don't know Charlotte and as I can neither read or write myself ……,"

He stopped and shrugged his shoulders. "I began to hope though," he said suddenly, "at the end of last summer. I shouldn't be telling you this, but she sent you a gown, a beautiful yellow gown. You did receive it didn't you?"

"But there was no note with it!" Charlotte exclaimed. "I could never understand why it was delivered to me. When I questioned the woman who delivered it, she would only say that it came from a dressmaker in Camelford; that she knew nothing more."

"That's what your mother asked her to say Charlotte. She didn't want you to know that she'd sent it. She tired of being a schoolmistress more than two years back, and she told me that she'd always wanted to train to be a dressmaker. And so that is what she did. She made tops and skirts, work dresses, bonnets and caps, but your dress was her first gown, designed just for you. She said that you would love the colour."

"She was right." Charlotte fell silent for a little while, struggling to understand what this new knowledge might mean. Was her mother ready now to have her home again? "Do you think that you could try again for me?" she asked him. "And I need you to tell her that I understand now and that I'll cause her no trouble. Just that. I must leave now or I'll not be back by morning. My master doesn't know that I have his horse or my mistress that I have her coat."

"And you say that you'll cause your mother no trouble!" He sounded serious but his eyes were smiling at her.

"Well maybe just a little," she said as she left him. "Maybe just a little from time to time!"

As Charlotte approached the kitchen door, it was suddenly flung open and she came face to face with her mistress, lighted candle in her hand. Mrs Peter, was looking absolutely furious as she stood in the entrance, completely blocking Charlotte's way back into the house.

"Where have you been Charlotte?" she demanded. "Riding off into the night like that with your master's horse, without a word to anyone. You've had us all up half the night and worried sick!"

"I'm sorry mistress, I didn't mean to disturb everyone's sleep, but I had to try and get word to my mother."

Seeing Charlotte's stricken face was enough to make her mistress stand back a little from the door and allow the girl to enter the kitchen. But she was still looking very angry.

"Will heard someone outside and he saw you from the window, leading Hercules out of the yard. He woke John but it was too late. By the time they got downstairs, you'd gone. Will's still out there now somewhere with Matthew, searching for you. If you wanted to get word to your mother, why ever didn't you ask one of the men to take her a letter? I'm sure they would have been more than willing. You've got them mooning around after you most of the time as it is. Poor love sick fools! Well I've had enough now Charlotte and that's a fact. I've always done my best for you and this is how you repay me. First setting the men folk against each other, and now stealing my John's horse and going off like that, frightening us all near to death. I'm sorry to have to say this, but I'm going to have to let you go Charlotte. Come Lady Day I'm going to give you notice to leave. You can stay here and work for as long as it takes you to find another position."

Her voice softened a little as she said, "I'm not going to throw you out with nowhere to go. There's times you've been like a daughter to me. But now, well I think it's best you go, and the farther away the better, for all our sakes."

Mrs Peter was true to her word. With the money she received fortnightly on a Monday, Charlotte was given her notice. She was no longer wanted in the house that she had called her home for the best part of seven years. Turning the coins over and over in her hand, four precious shillings, including two of her favourite little four penny pieces; money that she would be needing soon, one way or another.

That same day she noticed a stranger outside in the yard with her master, Will and Matthew.

"That'll be John Stevens," her mistress told her when she asked who the young man might be. "He'll be living here now; sleeping in with the master and Matthew. Will's to go home each night, back with

194

Isaac and Mary. John Stevens is here to help with the heavy work. He's a cousin to Will; Isaac's sister's boy; so he's family. I told Matthew of my intentions at the start of the month. I'll not have him coming to any harm while he's carrying out his work here."

"So that was Matthew Weeks," John Stevens remarked to Will, as they left Matthew working in the barn and went off around the fields with their master. John Peter had insisted on showing his new servant around the farm. "What's so special about him then, that I'm hired to save him from the hard work? Is he family too?"

"No, Matthew's not family John," Will told him, "But he came here on Lady Day seven years ago and the mistress thinks highly of him. He's not been well this year and she's looking out for him, that's all. He's got skills has Matthew. He's a good carpenter and he's had training as a blacksmith. He's clever."

"Not like me then," John Stevens grinned at Will. "Looks like I've come to work at the right farm though don't it? A caring mistress and a real pretty milkmaid about the place."

"It'll do you no good looking in her direction John!" Will grinned back at him. "She's been Matthew's girl for as long as I can remember!"

"I'll have to keep my eye on him then Will. Reckon I could learn a thing or two from Matthew Weeks."

Late that evening as Matthew was upstairs getting ready for bed, John Stevens walked into the room. He threw his jacket down on the floor and stood watching Matthew fold his clothes, before placing them neatly on top of his bed box.

"I could do with one of those boxes," he said, and before Matthew could stop him, he bent down and opened the lid, scattering the folded shirt and trousers down onto the bare floor boards. "Will said you're a carpenter. Could you make me one like this? I've not got as many clothes as this though; two good jackets and look at this fancy waistcoat!" He pulled the waistcoat out to look at it, revealing Charlotte's yellow gown, doubled over at the bottom of the box. "Why've you got a dress in with your things?" He was looking at Matthew in astonishment, waiting for an answer.

"It's Charlotte's dress John. We're courting. Will said that he told you. There's no room in her own small box for the dress, so I keep it for her, along with some of her other best clothes. It's no secret."
Matthew was finding John Stevens' obvious interest in him quite amusing. He might have to be more careful though. He didn't like people knowing too much of his business.

On the following Thursday Matthew was stacking wood behind the barn in the mowhay. Tom Prout came walking around from the side of the house.
"Thought I heard somebody back here," he said. "I was hoping to see John." He was looking wary; keeping his distance.
"Hoping to see Charlotte more like!" The words were out before he could stop himself. He had meant to be straight with Tom when he saw him again; tell him that Charlotte wanted to talk to him. But now that the man was standing there in front of him, Matthew knew that he still wanted to fight for her. Why should he help Tom Prout to take her away from him?
"Well what if I do want to see Charlotte? Where is she? She's not in the kitchen."
"She's not here. The mistress sent her out on an errand. I don't know where she's gone."

"I've had enough of this. I'm thinking of moving here to work Matthew and if I do, I'm going to take that girl away from you."

"And what makes you think you can do that? You've always had your eye on her, but she's not with you yet Tom Prout and she never will be. Not if I've got anything to do with it!"

"We'll see Matthew, we'll see. I know what that girl wants!" Tom turned on his heels and walked away, with Matthew still shouting after him.

John Stevens quietly closed the kitchen door that led out into the mowhay. He had heard their raised voices from inside the house and opened the door a little to listen in on the argument; but he wasn't the only one who had heard them. Phillipa Peter quietly closed Charlotte's bedroom window. She would have to try and find that girl another position. There would be no peace around the place until she was gone.

Tom wandered away from Penhale and took the lane towards the Chapman's place. He couldn't think of anywhere else nearby that his aunt might send Charlotte on an errand. He wasn't going back to Helset until he'd seen her. If she didn't want him he would have to go away again, but he had to know the truth.

Charlotte was wandering back to Penhale from John Chapman's farmhouse. Her mistress had run out of butter, and she'd been sent to see if Tamson had any to spare. The basket on her arm was full; not only with butter but with biscuits and jam as well.

She saw Tom walking towards her, hands in his pockets, looking down at the ground and aimlessly kicking stones about. She set down the basket. "Tom! You came back!" And running straight into his

197

outstretched arms, she was swept up and spun around and around until she had to beg him to put her down.

"I knew it," he said, gazing down at her. "I knew it!"

As they made their way back to Penhale she told him how desperate she had been; how she'd taken John's horse and ridden off to try to talk with her mother, and how she'd been given her notice, but didn't have to leave until she found a new position.

"Don't worry," he said, "we'll find somewhere. We can go somewhere together."

He left her just out of sight of the farmhouse. "Give me a week or two," he told her. "I'll sort this out I promise, and I'll come back for you."

That evening John Peter walked to Trevillian's Gate with Will to see Isaac and go for a drink at the Britannia Inn. With their master away, John Stevens sat talking with Matthew on the settle.

"I heard you and that Tom Prout arguing in the mowhay earlier today." John kept his voice down. "What makes him think that he can just move in here and take Charlotte from you? I haven't ever met with him but Will says he's his cousin."

"Oh, you're all related John, as far as I can see. All of you except for me and Charlotte. But if he comes here to live then I shall move out, for we never could agree, not since we lived together the last time." And not wanting John to know any more of his business than that, Matthew took off his boots and went up over the stairs to bed.

Sunday 31st March, 1844

When Matthew returned from his mother's house on the last Sunday in March, it was late in the afternoon. Phillipa Peter was relieved to see him come through the door. He had walked to Larrick on the Saturday and spent the night there, before walking back again to Penhale, but nevertheless it was a long way for him to travel on foot after his recent illness.

"I've saved you some dinner," she told him, "you must be starving," and soon he was tucking into a cold but tasty meal of beef and potatoes. He was quiet, tired she thought, but still she badgered him for news of his family and was told that his mother and little sisters were well, and that Janey was living near Plymouth Hoe and expecting her first child within the month. John Stevens was lounging in the window seat, idly listening to their conversation, until he saw Matthew pull a newspaper out of his bag and pass it over to Mrs Peter.

"Mother gave me this paper," he was saying. "There's a story in there about a James Medland, held in prison for murder. Isn't that the name of Charlotte's father; up at Tresparrett Post?"

John Stevens got up from his seat in the window and joined them at the table. "What's all this?" he asked. "Is Charlotte's father a murderer?"

"Well someone gave it to mother because they knew I worked with Charlotte, but as we couldn't read it, I brought it back for Charlotte to see. Has she gone to chapel?"

"Yes, she walked up with Will, but I'm not expecting her back until late. She's visiting with Tamson Chapman after the service. Let me have a look at that paper Matthew; see if I can make any sense of it." But all she could tell them was that the man in prison for murder was indeed a James Medland, and that he was being supported by his daughter.

When Charlotte came back at eight o'clock, they gave her the paper to read and at first she looked shocked, but then she began to laugh. "It's an old paper," she said. "See this at the top Matthew. It's dated July 1831. And it can't be the same man. I was almost five years old then and I've never heard any mention of it!"

Matthew was so tired that night that he went up to bed early, but sleep didn't come easily. It had been a good weekend; though his mother had cried when he told her of his long illness and the doctor's discovery of an irregular beat to his heart. And when he'd told her of his plans to leave Penhale farm; live at home again with her, and go back to his trade as a carpenter, the tears had flowed again; but that time, they'd been tears of joy and more than a little relief.

"Your uncle Richard would be only too glad to have you working with him again Matthew. I know I've told you this before son, but he's built that old carpentry business of his up again, and he's doing well with it. He had to pull himself together when your granddad died and he inherited the farm. In a way that farm saved him, helped him get through his grief, but he'll always be a carpenter at heart."

When Matthew finally drifted into a deep sleep that night, his dreams were all of a new and happy life.

Easter Monday 8th April, 1844

"Old Charles Parson's is in the yard, if you want to see what he's brought us." Mrs Peter was talking to Charlotte, but John Stevens went over to look out onto the yard from the kitchen window.

"No, I'll not go out today. He always encourages me to buy something from him. I must save my money now."

Charlotte had that day received her fortnightly dues; five shillings including one of her favourite silver fourpenny pieces. Just as soon as she could go upstairs, she would put the money away in her bedroom box.

John watched as probably the oldest man that he had ever seen, sat sifting through a large box, on the back of his cart. Matthew was with him, holding up a pair of fancy looking braces; but he dropped them as Charles Parsons handed him a middle sized kitchen knife. The blade glinted in the soft morning light as Matthew turned it over in his hands.

"That old man's got a good looking kitchen knife out there mistress. You might want to look at it."

"Thank you John but my John prefers to buy everything at the markets." She was finding it difficult at times, with two Johns in the house, especially since Isaac's young nephew seemed to have little sense when it came to realising who she was addressing.

"I think Matthew's bought it for himself," John Stevens remarked, watching money change hands outside.

"Well he needs a knife for his work," his mistress remarked, as Matthew came in through the door and went up over the stairs, carrying something to his room.

Saturday 13th April, 1844

Almost four weeks had passed since Ben Kircher had offered Charlotte a new life; staying for as long as she wished on his farm at Trebarwith, living with him and her sister Unity.

"If you decide to come with me," he'd said, *"meet up with me, four weeks from today. But if you're not here, I'll understand."*

And although she now felt that she didn't want to take up that offer, she did want to see him to explain, and arrange to somehow meet him again one day. It would mean though, that she had to walk out to Roughtor Ford on her own. She couldn't ask Matthew to go with her, for she would have to tell him soon that she had chosen Tom. More than two weeks had passed since she had met Tom in the lane near the Chapman's farm. He had promised to come back for her, but she'd had no word from him; and no word either from her mother.

It had been a fine, dry day and although it was now early evening, it was still warm outside, the yard bathed in a bright sunlight. Matthew was standing in the porch way with his razor and a hone, shadowed as usual by John Stevens.

"Watch what you're doing with that cut-throat Matthew! There's already a sweet edge on that blade!"

Simon Baker had joined them in the porch, holding a little parcel in his hand.

"Not as sweet as I'd like it," grumbled Matthew, "this hone's too hard to do a good job."

"Simon! This is a surprise." Phillipa Peter had heard his voice and gone bustling to the door.

"What's this you've brought us?" she asked; her eyes on the parcel.

"A delivery." He stepped into the kitchen and turning away from her, handed the parcel to Charlotte.

"I met a lady with a pony and trap in the lane; said she had a delivery for you Charlotte. A bonnet cap apparently." He gave her a sly little wink. "I said I'd take it from her; save her the trouble of coming all the way down here. Oh, and she told me that there's a letter with it."

"Where've you ordered a bonnet cap from Charlotte? They've never sent someone all the way out here from Camelford for the price of a bonnet cap!"

But Charlotte had gone; snatched the letter from Simon Baker's hand and run off up over the stairs.

"Well I never!" Phillipa declared. "That girl's turned quite wild of late Simon. I don't know what to make of her anymore!"

Upstairs in her room Charlotte sat on the bed, her hands shaking. Simon Baker had brought her a letter from her mother, disguised for some reason as a delivery of a bonnet cap. There had been no lady in the lane with a pony and trap. She was sure of it. She tore open the parcel. There was a letter, tucked carefully inside a pretty lace bonnet cap. She read ……

My Dear Charlotte,
James has just told me of your surprise visit to us. I do so wish that I had been here, but I only returned today from staying with Margaret, as he explained to you. She gave birth to a beautiful baby girl and all is well, so I was able to leave them.

What can I say to you my darling girl, except that you must come home as soon as possible? James gave me your message, though he said it made no sense to him. He says that you are delightful, and he looked so happy Charlotte, when I said that I would write and ask you to come back to us. I am putting my trust in you now child. Come home.

Since it seems that you were unable to tell the Peters that you wanted to visit us, and that you are no longer happy there, I thought it best that Simon brought you this letter under the pretence that it is a delivery. If it would help, he is prepared to ask Mrs Peter to release you from her service and to bring you home. He seems to think there will be no problem with this.

We hope to see you soon Charlotte.
Mother.

She could go home. Her mother was trusting her to say nothing to James of any other father, and she was asking her to return to her home. Of course they didn't realise that she had already received her notice, and that it wouldn't be at all difficult for her to leave Penhale. She would go out on the moor tomorrow at five o'clock to see her father, and when she returned she would speak with her mistress. There was a chance that if she told her tonight, her mistress would send her straight home in the morning, with John Peter in the horse and cart. She couldn't risk that. She had to meet her father to explain and to tell him her good news.

Sunday 14th April, 1844

Unable to sleep at all during the night, Charlotte arose early to help her mistress with the milking. Phillipa Peter was longing to ask her about the letter that had come with the bonnet cap, and indeed, how she had managed to order the cap in the first place, but Charlotte had been distant with her since receiving her notice, and so she felt that it might be easier to say nothing about it. The girl had remained friendly, but had seemed reluctant to answer her questions; often not replying at all or somehow turning the conversation around.

The weather had changed. The day was damp and foggy and as Phillipa went about her work, collecting all the dirty clothes and bed linen, ready for the Monday morning wash, she was hoping for better weather for the drying over the next few days. Knowing that Matthew was up in his bedroom, she sent Charlotte up with his clean shirt for the week ahead.
"I've laid out his blue stockings on his bed box," she called after her from the bottom of the stairs, and she noticed that Charlotte was checking the stitching on the collar of the shirt, as she knocked on the boys' bedroom door. It was the shirt that the girl had mended herself after Thomas had ripped it apart on the last day of March. Matthew must have opened the door to her because Phillipa heard him ask her if she could wash his waistcoat, and then Charlotte had gone into her own bedroom leaving the door ajar.

Charlotte had read her mother's letter over and over again; and now, when she had meant to start changing her own bed for the Monday wash, she sat to read it again.

"Charlotte. I've brought you my waistcoat. What's that you've got there?" Matthew was standing in the doorway, waistcoat in his hand; staring at her letter.

"It's the letter that Simon Baker brought last night when he came with my parcel. It's from Rebecca; Rebecca Lanxon." She lied, not wanting anyone to know as yet that the letter had come from her mother. "You remember Matthew. I told you that she offered to find a position for me over in Blisland. Well she wants me to go there for a while and help her with her new baby, and then look for other work in the future. She says that they haven't as yet found a teacher for the new school house."

Matthew was looking at her in astonishment. "Simon Baker brought you a letter from Rebecca Lanxon? But he doesn't live anywhere near Blisland. How did he come by it?"

"I have no idea Matthew and I'd thank you not to say anything of it at the moment. I haven't decided what I'm going to do. It's too soon."

"Well, since you haven't seen anything of Tom and I've heard no mention of you going off to live with your father today, I'm hoping that you'll come away with me Charlotte." He moved further into the room and closed the door behind him. "I'm planning to go back to Larrick to live with my family, and work with my uncle Richard. We could get married Charlotte."

"Well I'm happy for you Matthew, truly I am, but I need just a few more hours before I can give you an answer. I am going to meet my father on the moor this afternoon, but I am not going away with him. I have at least decided that."

"I thought that you'd arranged not to meet him if you didn't want to live with him. I hope you're not expecting me to walk out there with you again? I'm not going to encourage you with this Charlotte. There's no need for it."

"I have my reasons for meeting him Matthew. I couldn't ask you to come with me. I knew how you would feel about it. I did think of asking John Prout, but I've not seen him around."

"John Prout? Why John Prout?"

"I knew he would go with me if I asked him, and I thought I could trust John, he's never really serious about anything, is he? He just makes me laugh."

She stood up and kissed him on the cheek.

"Will you give me just a few more hours to think about my answer? And don't worry about me walking out on the moor on my own. I'll be quite safe out there."

As he left the room she closed the door behind him and folded her letter, putting it into her apron pocket. It might be safer not to leave it in her room.

Later that morning as Charlotte and her mistress were preparing the dinner and Matthew and John Stevens sat drinking tea at the table, Tom Prout limped in through the door.

"Thomas!" Phillipa Peter was obviously delighted to see her nephew. "What's the matter with your leg? Sit down, sit down it must be painful!"

He grinned at her, rubbing his knee. "It's nothing," he said. "I fell off the old cart this morning. Fooling around with John; but it is painful!"

He sat on the settle for half an hour, talking to his aunt and drinking the tea that Charlotte took over to him, while Matthew sat watching and wondering what he could do to stop what he was sure was going to happen next.

When Tom left the kitchen, Charlotte followed him. Matthew could hear their voices as they stood talking, just out of sight, around to the back of the porch way, but try as he might, he could hear nothing of what was being said.

"I'm sorry I've not been back before now." Tom was looking relieved that she had followed him outside. "But I can't find anywhere nearby for us to work together. We might have to go away somewhere Charlotte."

She laughed and took the letter from her pocket.

"Simon Baker brought me this note from my mother last night. I'm going home Tom. I'll be living less than two miles from Helset. We'll be together soon!"

They fell silent as he took her into his arms.

"Have they gone away?" Matthew asked his mistress, as she too had seemed to be listening to the voices outside.

"What can they have to say to one another?"

"I could not tell," Mrs Peter replied, and so Matthew stood up and going out into the little porch, he leaned against the wall to try to listen.

"Can you meet me this afternoon?" Charlotte was saying, "Walk somewhere with me?"

"Oh my love, not this afternoon. I promised my brother that I would help him repair a wall. The bullocks are coming in from the moor and ruining his potato plot. But I'll meet you later at Tremail Chapel after evening service. Though I'll tell you now Charlotte, I'm not planning on walking far with you, not with this knee of mine. And I haven't waited this long for you, to waste any of our time walking!"

After dinner Phillipa Peter noticed Matthew outside, waving a piece of paper about in his hand. And then she saw that Charlotte was trying to catch it and take it from him. They are still very loving together she thought. In spite of all the disagreements, they are still very fond of each other.

Still fooling around with what looked now to be a letter, they came inside and went upstairs together.

"Why must you go to meet your father?" Matthew asked, as they reached the top of the stairs. "Don't go Charlotte!"

"We'll talk later," she said, "I have to go, and I don't want you to say that you will come with me. But you can do something for me. I couldn't rest at all last night. I need to sleep. Will you wake me before three o'clock? That will allow me plenty of time to walk out to Roughtor Ford. The moor will be wet, so I plan to wear my pattens."

There was no one in his bedroom, so Matthew went in to lie on his bed. He had to do something. He couldn't let Charlotte walk out on the moor on her own. He had promised himself that he would never let that happen. Whenever he remembered the day that they had first walked out to Roughtor, he could still feel her little arms around his neck, her legs dangling around his sides as he carried her back to the farmhouse.

"Please don't ever leave me out here on the moor alone,"

she had begged him. He wasn't going to break that promise, even though he was sure that he had lost her to Tom. And then there was this business of her father. She didn't really know him. What if he were to force her to go with him? If she met him out there on her own, they might never see her again. Losing her to Tom was nothing compared to that. But that wasn't going to happen either. Not if there was something that he could do to try to stop it.

Taking his pocket watch out, he studied the time. It was half the hour past one o'clock. Carefully, he wound the hands around until they were reading half the hour past twelve o'clock again. When he woke Charlotte and showed her the time, telling her that it was almost three o'clock, it would be almost four o'clock. He was going with her out to Roughtor, and if he was fortunate, she would be too late to meet her father. He would be gone, thinking that his daughter had made other plans. And she would be too late as well to meet Tom. The man would go back to Helset, thinking that she had changed her mind about him, and by the time he returned to Penhale, Charlotte would no longer be there. For he planned to take her with him to Larrick to live with his mother. They would be gone before the week was out. He would marry her as soon as it could be arranged. His mistress would release him from her service. She had already promised to do that whenever he wished it.

When he woke her, she was surprised to see that he was in his Sunday best; dressed to go out.
"I'll walk with you a little way," he said, "As far as Higher Down Gate but then I'll take the road past Sam Prout's. I plan to go up to Halworthy."
"But that's out of your way Matthew. You could cross the fields through Great Well meadow and reach the road far sooner!"
"I've said I'll walk near to the edge of the moor with you Charlotte. I'll not change my mind now!"

It was close to the hour of four in the afternoon when Matthew came down over the stairs, a little ahead of Charlotte, and passed straight through the kitchen, out into the porch. He was hoping that Charlotte would quickly follow him, so that there would be no

210

questions from his mistress, nor any mention of the time. But Mrs Peter had spotted them.

"Where are you going at this time Charlotte? You are too late for afternoon service and too early for preaching in the evening."

Matthew waited with baited breath, but Charlotte made no reply to the question, and came out to him in the porch.

"What can I say to her?" she asked him. "She is asking me where I am going!"

"Tell her that you will not be back in time to milk the cows, but that I will be. That's her only reason for asking Charlotte; you can be sure of it."

John Stevens, who was passing the porch on his way to the stable, and as always, minding Matthew's business in place of his own, asked him why he had thrown away so much money on a new cloth coat, when the dark velvet one that he was wearing was perfectly good. Matthew was saved from answering, as Charlotte returned from the kitchen. Watched by John Stevens, and John Peter who was across the yard tending the pigs, the couple set out on their journey through the farmyard and toward the lane that led to Higher Down Gate.

"Fine looking maid," John Stevens remarked to his master. "I'd ask her to keep company with me if she weren't Matthew's girl."

"They're close; but I'm not so sure where it's headin'."

John Peter returned to his pigs.

It was a good half hour walk to Higher Down Gate. The day was still dirty, foggy and damp. Charlotte had been grateful to share the umbrella that Matthew always took with him on his long journeys, even on fine days; it was a good walking aid.

"I'll not need the umbrella. I've got my bonnet and you'll need it yourself if you're going all the way to Halworthy."

She was though, half hoping that he'd lend it to her; since she'd been hiding behind it as they neared the gate. Her journey was taking her past Samuel Prout's home, and close to Isaac Cory's. Tom had told her that he was helping Samuel repair the wall to his potato plot, so she knew that he was somewhere nearby. The last thing that she wanted was for Tom to see her with Matthew, or, to see her walking out on the moor on her own.

"I'm not going to Halworthy," he said. "I'm coming with you to meet your father."

"Matthew, I do not want you to go any further."

"I'll not let you go out there on your own Charlotte, and if truth were told, you would much rather have my company. Am I right?"

Reluctantly she nodded. As long as Tom didn't see them together, she would be thankful for Matthew's company. She would keep the umbrella over her head, and hope that the fog would thicken.

As they made their way out onto the moor, neither of them noticed that Isaac Cory was watching. He was on his way home from the afternoon service at Davidstow church and had stopped to look at his wheat field. From where he stood, he could see the moor just beyond Higher Down Gate and noticed two people walking steadily in the direction of Lanlary Rock. He was certain that one was a woman, for he could see what looked like a red shawl, and that she was sheltering under an umbrella. The other was a man. He couldn't see him at all well, but it was clear that he was limping quite badly.

The preacher William Gard was also crossing Bodmin moor that same afternoon. He was on his way home at around five thirty when he spotted two people walking near to Roughtor ford but going towards Lanlary Rock. Neither Charlotte nor Matthew noticed him however, as Charlotte was upset at not finding her father by the river; although, as Matthew pointed out, it was not yet five o'clock by his pocket watch.

It was about an hour later however, nearer to half the hour past six o'clock, that Charlotte did see someone that she knew. She had been pacing to and fro on the moor, watching the ford, with Matthew following her, when, as they were turning towards the ford she saw a horse and rider about a quarter of a mile from them.
"Oh my lord Matthew; it's Richard Pethick!"
"What does that matter? I thought he was your friend."
"He is, but if he recognises me he will stop to talk and, well Matthew, you don't know him, but he will talk forever. And if my father comes, Richard will want to talk to him as well. I won't be able to speak with my father on my own. Matthew! He mustn't see me!"
"He's coming closer now; so keep the umbrella over your head. He doesn't know me, and I won't speak to him. He'll soon ride off."

Charlotte walked a little way away; the umbrella covering her face.
"Are you afraid of each other?" Richard called out. He'd been watching them from more than a mile away, to-ing and fro-ing; sometimes together, sometimes apart, and now the man was just a stone's throw away, and looking straight towards him.
"Have you lost yourselves?" he asked, but as Matthew didn't reply, he continued on his way.

"He's gone Charlotte." Matthew walked over to her. "He'll be right away from us in a few minutes."

"I should not have done that to him," she said. "He's a dear young man, but I felt I had no choice."

"No one's ever told me that it is difficult to stop him from talking."

"Well mention it to the mistress, she'll tell you. She's very fond of him, but she says that you need half a day with nothing to do, to speak with Richard Pethick! My father's not coming Matthew. It's too late now. It must be well past six o'clock, and it's growing dark already. We'll make our way back."

"It is dark tonight, but it's been a dirty day," he replied. "I'll go to the bridge and have one last look for him before we go." He was hoping to delay her for just a little longer. As she watched him walk slowly away, Charlotte took off her bonnet and cap, shaking out her dark hair, so that it fell down around her shoulders. It would curl up now in the damp air and look unruly and wild, but she didn't care. Tom would like it like that. She dropped her bag and her shawl, took off her gloves and the little collar that was around her neck, undoing some of the buttons at the front of her dress. The little river looked inviting. She would splash her face in the clean cold water and walk a little way along its course. Taking off her pattens and shoes, she walked to the water's edge. Tonight she would give herself to Tom. She knew now that she had only been waiting for the right man; waiting for him.

"Charlotte! Whatever are you doing now?" Matthew was clambering down the little bank towards her. "There's no one to be seen." His face was white and he seemed to slip, but then he fell like a stone down onto his back. He wasn't moving. She ran to him.

"Matthew, Matthew! Not here! Please get up Matthew!"

She dropped to her knees beside him, bending over a little to make sure that he was breathing. He was!

As she started to loosen his collar she heard a horse somewhere, up in the trees behind the bank, and then heavy boots running up behind her.

"Richard!" she called out, "Thank God you came back. It's Matthew. I can't ....."

But he had caught hold of her by her hair and was pulling her up and away to one side. She struggled, holding on fiercely to Matthew's collar and ripping it. It was then that she felt a blow on the back of her neck and saw blood fly out in front of her, some of it splashing onto the cuff of Matthew's sleeve.

"Lord help me!" She felt another blow to her neck and for a second she saw the hand that took her life, and in that second she understood, and knew that it wasn't Richard Pethick.

When Matthew came around, he scrambled to his feet, trying once more to regain his senses. Where was Charlotte? And then he saw her, lying beside the course of the river, her face looking up towards the sky, her dress dirtied and open at the front as if she had rolled towards the river. Her throat had been horribly cut! He fell onto the ground, clutching at his own throat. Who had done this? Her broken coral necklace was resting behind her but some of its beads lay in a trail, leading back towards the bank where he had fallen in a faint. Half walking, half crawling, he followed their path to where pools of blood were trickling, spreading slowly outwards through the granite stones. Charlotte's blood! Hit by a sudden, irrational rage, he took his whittling knife from the pocket of his jacket and stabbed furiously at the turf on the bank, cutting earth away until he had made a small pit. Frantically scooping up pools of blood with his bare hands, he threw them into the pit until he could do no more; and so he scraped some of the earth back into the pit to fill it again, and covered it over with the piece of turf. His hands! They were caked with earth, and beneath that with blood. He would have to clean them before he went back to the farmhouse and so, very slowly, he returned to the river and knelt beside her body to wash in the river water. He could hardly bear to look at her. His precious girl! He had buried her blood, but he couldn't bury her. How could he leave her there? All alone on the moor! But if he believed, as she had believed, then the real Charlotte was no longer lying there beside him; she was with the angels.

His hands were clean again and the river had washed away the fresh blood on the edge of his shirt sleeve. As he stood up to leave her he saw the clothes and shoes that she had dropped near the bank. He had to take them; to keep at least a little part of her with him. At first he walked backwards, slowly and carefully, still watching her, carrying everything that she had left near the bank. But then he turned and ran, as fast as he could, back towards Lower Penhale farm. He had been running for several minutes before he caught his foot in an old turf pit and fell headlong, his body sprawled out on the rough grass; Charlotte's belongings scattered around him. He lay there, the breath knocked out of him, but the fall had somehow brought back his reason. He couldn't be seen with Charlotte's clothes. If anyone knew that he had been on the moor with her that day, he would hang for her murder! The only person to see them together had been Richard Pethick, but Richard didn't know him, and hadn't recognised Charlotte. He should be quite safe with that. Picking up her bonnet cap, her little bag and her gloves, he hid them around his person and placed the rest of her belongings in the old turf pit, covering them over with moss. Walking the rest of the way, he was back on the farm by nine thirty that evening.

Only his mistress looked up as he walked through the door and into the kitchen. His master was at the table and John Stevens on the settle. He crossed the room to sit in his window seat.

"Where's Charlotte?" Mrs Peter asked after a while.

"I don't know where she is," he replied.

"You always say that Matthew, and then she comes in soon after you. I dare say she's gone to the barn to see the dogs! She ought to have come straight in and fetched you some supper."

"I won't bother with supper tonight," he said; but she sighed and got up from the table to get him a meal.

Thankfully, he thought, the room was quite dark, lit only by the candles on the table.

"Where is Charlotte, then? " John Peter asked him.

"I can't say. She may have met up with Tom Prout or else his brother John"

Somehow he ate his supper and then sat for a while, staring out into the darkness. Had Tom killed Charlotte? He had heard him say that he would be at his brother Sam's in the afternoon. Had he seen them go out onto the moor; followed and found them together by the river? Had he thought the worst of her and ………? But to think that was madness. If he had followed them, they would have seen him. And Tom couldn't have killed Charlotte. He loved her. Besides, it wasn't in him. There was no real malice in Tom Prout. The man would sooner slope off back to Helset

217

for a week or two. He knew Tom. An old enemy, but not one to fear.

At half the hour past ten he took off his boots, put them under the chair by the stairs and went up to bed. Phillipa Peter waited a while longer for Charlotte to come back. Where was the girl? Isaac had called in on them earlier that evening and mentioned that he'd seen two people walking on the moors. He'd been looking at his wheat, he'd said and thought it might have been Matthew out there with a woman, since the man had a bad limp. She hadn't taken too much notice of what he'd been saying. She knew that Isaac's sight was so bad that he couldn't have known it was Matthew out there; but then he told her that the woman was wearing a red shawl and had also been wearing pattens, and that he knew this because he'd followed the track that the couple had taken, and seen recent patten marks. Charlotte had been wearing pattens and a red shawl. Had Matthew and Charlotte walked out onto the moor in that dirty weather?
You may have seen Matthew out there with Charlotte she'd told Isaac. But she may have walked out there with Thomas. I saw her with him in the yard this morning, and he's limping bad himself. Fell off a cart over at Rosebenault.
"Set her sights on our Tom then has she?" he'd asked. *"I thought there was something going on there, as far back as Christmas."*

Matthew had left the farmhouse with Charlotte, but returned without her, and hadn't Charlotte said herself that she wouldn't be back to milk the cows, but that Matthew would. The girl had certainly had plans that didn't involve Matthew. It was late. She was tired and could wait for Charlotte no longer. The door would be open if she chose to return.

Although Matthew was up early next morning and out of bed before John Stevens, he sat on his bed so long, that both Johns were down in the kitchen before him.

"Matthew!" His mistress was calling him from the bottom of the stairs. "Are you coming down to help me milk? Charlotte's not back, so I've no one to help me today. You must help, for this is your doing, I'm sure of it; her disappearing in this way!"

So soon! Charlotte had gone and it was his doing! He hadn't slept all night for grief and worry and now she was blaming him; although all he had said was that he didn't know where she was.

While he helped her with the milking, she questioned him still, insisting that he must know where she was. But later, when he asked if he could have Charlotte's clothes from her bedroom box, she let him take the box into the empty middle room. He left it there, but took some of her best clothes from it; her best yellow gown, the new bonnet cap and a silk handkerchief. He'd had to leave most of her clothes on the moor, but he could take at least some comfort from having these near him. He put them in his own bedroom box.

When Mary arrived to visit her mother, he heard her ask where Charlotte was.

"Only Matthew knows that," she'd said, "for he went away with her, and returned without her."

After dinner his mistress had found his blue stockings and asked him why they were so dirty at the front. It was as if he'd been cutting turf on the moor, she'd said. And later that day, when Mary had gone home and he was alone with her in the kitchen, she'd questioned him again, about where Charlotte was.

"Has she gone to her mother's again, and asked you not to tell?"

"No mistress," he'd said, weary of her badgering. *"She went out on the moor. I left her at Higher Down Gate since she didn't want me going any further with her. I walked up to Halworthy to visit with Mary and John, but as they didn't answer their door, I called at Sarah Westlake's house."*

He was hoping that his story would stop her questions for a while; that she would believe that he had no knowledge of Charlotte's whereabouts. But Phillipa Peter was now very worried. Isaac had said that he'd seen Matthew starting out on the moor with a woman. If the man with the limp wasn't Matthew, then who was it? Had she gone off somewhere with Thomas?

The next day over breakfast John Stevens had stirred the business up again. *"I see your shirt is ripped at the collar Matthew, and the button missing. Is that the shirt that was mended before? It must have been badly mended."*

"Twas not badly mended!" Mrs Peter cut in on their conversation. *"The stitching was firm enough. What have you been doing to rip it at the collar Matthew?"* And then, before they had finished their breakfast she was at him again. *"What's Charlotte's pretty lace cap doing out on the thorn Matthew? That was never there earlier! You come and take it in, for you must have put it there!*

"I'll come and drag it in! he'd said to her, angry that no one would leave him be. Giving him one of her looks, she fetched it in herself, and grumbled that it had been badly washed. He'd washed it himself; swishing

220

it about outside in the water trough, along with his soiled best waistcoat; hiding the cap inside the waistcoat in case anyone had asked him what he was doing there. Lying as it had been on the bank of the river, it had been reached by a trickling pool of blood. He'd thought that his mistress would think that Charlotte had left it outside, along with his waistcoat. Later in the day he'd noticed her bring that in off the hedge and she'd washed it again. But she'd said no more to him.

He couldn't turn around for people questioning him. He was working in the mowhay when Elias Bettison turned up at his side.
"They tell me she's gone boy", he'd said. *"Where's she gone then?"* It was to be expected that the old man would ask, so, making light of it, he'd told him that he didn't know and asked if Elias knew where they could find another maid. *"Poor, friendless young girl,"* the old man had said, *"I've heard her mother's against her!"* And, angry at the mention of Charlotte's mother, he'd almost let it slip that Charlotte was no longer alive. *"I've heard that too,"* he'd said, *"and that her mother would kill her if she came inside her door. If Charlotte's found dead, it should be her mother that's tried for her life!"*

Afterwards, when he went back inside the house, his mistress had tackled him again. *"I overheard you talking with old Elias in the mowhay,"* she'd told him. *"You have worried me now Matthew. If you don't tell me where Charlotte is, I will apply to a magistrate this very day and tell all of this."*

He'd panicked then. He would have to tell her something. And he'd thought of the letter Charlotte

221

had received from Rebecca Lanxon. That should silence her for a while.

"If you must know the truth," he'd said, *"she's gone to Blisland to help Rebecca Lanxon with her new baby. Rebecca sent her a letter and Charlotte said that since you'd given her notice to leave, she would go to Blisland and that it would be an easier position. She intended sleeping at Hezekiah Spear's at Brown Willy overnight, as it was too far to walk on Sunday night."*

But his mistress would not let it go. *"And how did she get that letter? I gave her notice on Lady Day,"* she'd said, *"but we'd not mentioned it since. Why did she not tell me that she was leaving my service and why did she walk to Rebecca's in just the clothes she stood up in? It's ten miles to Blisland! We would have helped her to go to Rebecca's if she had asked. I would have approved of that. It's a very suitable position for her."*

She had seemed angry with him then, not answering when he spoke to her, and so in the evening, when they were all together in the kitchen, he asked John Stevens if he had a needle and thread, as he wished to sew the button on his shirt. John offered him a needle, but it was rusty, and the only thread he'd had was dark.

"Matthew, I'll sew the button on for you with good white cotton," his mistress had interrupted their conversation. *"But I'll only do it if you'll help me milk."* He hadn't replied for he'd guessed that she only wanted to question him again, and she hadn't waited long for an answer. *"You've put Charlotte away like this,"* she scolded him. *"It's jealousy that's done it; but there are men in Blisland as well as here Matthew. It'll do you no good."* He'd protested but there was no stopping it now. John Stevens had asked how far he'd

walked with Charlotte. *"You were seen on the moor together,"* he'd said. John Peter had joined in then. *"Isaac Cory saw you beyond Higher Down Gate."*
"No one saw me and no one spoke to me."

On Friday morning Matthew lay awake, long before dawn, struggling to make some sense of the last few days. He felt that he had no one here now who was a true friend. A true friend would have trusted him, even if they hadn't really believed the stories he was telling. Charlotte would have trusted him; put her arm around him and laid her head on his shoulder; helped him to find a way through his troubles. It had always been that way, since the first day that she came to live at the farm, when he had helped her, stemmed her tears. From then on they had looked after each other. But he had let her down on her last day; tricked her to keep her from her father and from Tom Prout. His hadn't been the hand that took her life, but without his trickery she would have still been alive; probably alive and in the arms of Tom Prout, but he blamed himself now, at least in part, for Charlotte's death.

Long before the other members of the household were awake, he dressed and went down into the kitchen, made himself something to eat and went outside to start on the day's work.
"Where's Matthew this morning?" Phillipa Peter asked her son finding him with John Stevens down in the kitchen before her.
"Gone out already." It was John Stevens who answered her. "He's eaten before us," and he pointed at an empty plate beside some butter and a loaf of bread, left uncovered on the table.

"So, he's avoiding us now is he?" Phillipa pursed her lips, "Well what does he plan to do about his dinner I wonder?"

Matthew did have plans for his dinner. Around mid-morning he went into his woodshed and, unlocking his toolbox, removed all the tools to reach the false floor that he had built into it. It was beneath that false floor that he kept his money; his wages when he was given them, and the five pounds that he had inherited from his Grandfather. Taking out some coins, he replaced everything, locked up the box and returned to the yard, jiggling the coins around in his hand.

"What's that you've got there?" John Stevens was at his side and saw the coins, including three little silver fourpenny pieces. "Is that Charlotte's money? She had three of those four penny pieces paid to her in her dues. She showed them to me. Said they were her favourites."

"Yes," Matthew told him, afraid that John might begin to guess where he kept his money, if he said that they were his own coins. "They were Charlotte's coins. Before she left, she asked me to lend her half a crown, but I needed some money for myself and offered her one and sixpence. She gave me these coins for the change. I like to be given fourpenny pieces," he added, laughing and hoping to lead the conversation away from Charlotte. "They will often do to pass as sixpences!"

At midday Matthew downed tools and walked to the Britannia Inn. He would have a drink and a pie there, well away from the farmhouse kitchen and the endless questions. It was two o' clock before he returned, his senses dulled from both beer and cider.

His master was in the yard beside the pig shed, with John Stevens and John Chapman the butcher.

"He has come back!" John Chapman was saying. "We've been waiting for you Matthew!" and opening the door to the piggery, he brought one of the animals out into the yard.

"Why waiting me?" Matthew asked him.

"When I was here last to kill a pig for your dinners, you told me that you'd do the job for me next time. Said you wanted to give it a try. Changed your mind have you?"

Matthew couldn't answer him. How could he kill a pig now? His hands began to shake.

"Come on boy," John Chapman was goading him. "My Tamson's been saying as how she thinks it's Tom Prout that's taken Charlotte away. Well this pig here is Tom Prout come back Matthew. What are you going to do about it?"

Enraged by John Chapman's words, Matthew took the little knife from his pocket and struck the pig with it. But his thrust was unsuccessful, and the butcher handed him a better knife for the job. This time the animal fell down dead in the yard; but it wasn't Tom Prout that Matthew had raised the knife to kill, or even the hapless animal; it was the person who had taken the life of Charlotte Dymond.

Nothing more was said to Matthew that day, but on the Saturday it became clear to him that he was the talk of the neighbourhood. He was working in Higher Down field with John Peter, when he saw William Hocken approaching from his own adjoining field.

"Matthew!" he called out, jumping over the hedge that separated them. "What's this I hear about Charlotte then? That you went away with her, but now she has disappeared."

225

"He's put her out on the moor," John Peter had said to William, "away from Tom Prout."

"Out on the moors!" William had said, as if he was joking.

"It's too cold to put her out summering with the animals yet!" But then the tone of his voice had suddenly changed. "I'm being serious with you now Matthew. Something is very wrong here. Have you put her out on the moor and destroyed her? She has been missing now for a week!"

"No, I have not! I have said that I left her, down there at the gate and that I walked up to Halworthy."

William had turned then and gone off across his fields, but John Peter must have told his mother of their conversation, for in the evening she tackled him with it.

"The neighbours are saying bad things about you Matthew," she'd said, "saying that you have destroyed that lovely girl. If they are right then you should be hung in chains."

Shocked to hear these words from the mistress he was so fond of, he'd crossed the room to get away from her, and stood by the kitchen dresser; his head bowed.

"Come back over here Matthew," she'd said, "I want to talk to you." But he'd unfastened his shoes; left them under the chair, and gone straight up to bed.

Sunday 21st April, 1844

One week had passed since Charlotte had walked away from Lower Penhale Farm and disappeared. It was early morning, before breakfast, that Phillipa asked Matthew for Charlotte's clothes.
"I'll keep them for the time being," she said, "until we find out more about this matter."
He said nothing over breakfast, or before going out to feed the bullocks, dressed as usual in his working clothes. It was time to find out the truth, and so, while he was outside, she asked her son and John Stevens to ride to Hezekiah Spear's and to George Lanxon's farm in Blisland. As she watched them ride away, Matthew returned to the kitchen and went straight upstairs, asking her nothing about their destination. When he came back down, she noticed that he was dressed in his best cloth coat and plain waistcoat; along with the best boots and trousers that he had worn when he had left the house with Charlotte, the week before. She asked him if he would be back for dinner and he said that he thought he would, or, if not then, soon afterwards. He had gone out to his woodshed then for a while, before setting off in the direction of Bodmin Moor.

Mary arrived later in the morning, to be told by her mother that she now suspected Matthew of having more to do with Charlotte's disappearance than he was telling.
"When I asked him where he was on Sunday afternoon, he told me that he'd gone up to visit with you and John. And then he said that since you weren't at home, he called on Sarah."

"But we were both at home mother. Don't you remember my telling you that I was not feeling well and neither was Sarah; but that she had the children with her as she always does on a Sunday. She said nothing to me of seeing Matthew!"

Phillipa was shocked. It seemed that Matthew had not been telling the truth and that Isaac may have been right about seeing him out on the moor.

"He's gone out for a while," she whispered, as if he might hear her. "Do you think we should search his bedroom?"

"I think we should certainly search his bedroom." Mary replied so loudly that Phillipa jumped.

Searching the pockets of Matthew's velvet jacket, they found his red cotton handkerchief, and a green gauze neckerchief, which Mary knew was Charlotte's, as she had borrowed it from her one cold night to wear on her journey home to Halworthy. Returning the kerchiefs to the pockets, they opened Matthew's bedroom box.

"Isaac's John saw him buy a knife from old Charles Parsons a while back, and he should have his razor in here somewhere." But the only thing of any note that they could find in the box was the newspaper with a story about a murder.

John Peter brought them disturbing news when he came back on his own in the afternoon. Hezekiah Spear had been at his home at Brown Willy from five o'clock onwards on that previous Sunday, and had seen nothing of Charlotte. And John Stevens brought a similar tale from Blisland. Rebecca had not sent any letter to Charlotte and, neither she nor George Lanxon, had seen or heard anything of her for months.

When Phillipa snuffed out the candles in the kitchen that night, Matthew had still not returned.

The next day found Phillipa searching the boys' bedroom again, but this time it was for the usual Monday wash. Collecting all their dirty clothes, she noticed that Matthew's shirt was missing. He was usually so tidy that she wondered if he had been wearing it when he went away, or if he had taken it with him. But then she spotted it, lying under his and John Stevens' bed. The button had been off on the previous Tuesday, she knew that, but now she could see that the collar had been torn away a little from the shirt, and that the pleats at the front were ripped apart. There were also a few small marks of blood on it.

Something had to be done, for she felt sure now that Charlotte had not simply left Penhale to go to another position; but that, as William Hocken had said to John, the girl had been put out on the moor and destroyed. She would arrange a search party for the very next day.

Sunday 28th April, 1844

It was a dry day, cool but sunny, and after dinner Unity Kircher had ridden the short distance to the coast on the fox coloured highland pony she'd owned since she was a child. She'd named him Romany, after her people, and proudly told that he had descended from a brave Spanish stallion who, generations before, had swum ashore after a shipwreck somewhere along Scotland's rocky coastline. This afternoon she'd ridden him for miles along grassy clifftops before heading back to their farm at Trebarwith.

She saw her father from two fields away, as he rode into the farmyard, dismounted and walked purposefully into the house, leaving his horse in the yard; not taking it to the stable as he normally did. Perhaps he was going out again. He had been different since he'd heard the news of Charlotte's death, sometimes he was angry, sometimes brooding, often blaming himself. He'd been in Tintagel on the Thursday, and heard that a search party had found the body of a young servant girl from Lower Penhale farm near Bodmin moor. Charlotte, they'd said her name was, Charlotte Dymond. A young man had been arrested in Plymouth, and brought before the magistrates that day up at Halworthy.

The next day the newspapers had the story and her father had come home from Camelford, thrown a paper down on the table and gone to sit in his chair by the fireplace.
"What's this father?" she asked him. "Why have you brought this paper back with you? We can't read it."

"They've arrested Matthew Weeks," he said, "that crippled boy. Charlotte was murdered and left out on the moor. Her funeral was yesterday. No friends there, no family to follow her. They were all up at Halworthy for the magistrates hearing."

He'd fallen silent then and not spoken to her for hours. The next day he'd ridden off to market, but not told her where. He'd come back in a stupor from drink with another paper; brought back he said from the pub. It seemed that someone had been standing, reading the story aloud, saying that the verdict of the inquest was wilful murder and that the case would go on to another court in Bodmin. The poor girl had struggled they'd said; there were bruises on her wrists and neck and her face was yellow from days in the sun.

As Unity rode into the farmyard, her father came out of the house.
"Stay on your horse daughter. We're leaving."
"Leaving father? Where are we going?"
"Back to our family; they'll be in Devon now. I know where to find them."
"But why father? Who will look after the horses? And I'll need to take my clothes."
"I've made arrangements. It's all taken care of, and you don't need anything. I'll buy you new clothes. I can't stay here Unity. I can't listen to all this talk about Charlotte. The case won't be tried for months and then all the talk will start again."
He must have seen the shock on her face as he mounted his horse, and turned it towards the gate.
"We'll come back daughter. We'll come back with a cart for our things. But not until this is over."

231

As he rode away, she stayed for while in the yard, looking at the house and the open door into the kitchen. But Romany turned, eager to chase her father's horse, and on her command they were quickly into a gallop; riding back to her own people.

Thursday April 25th 1844, was the day that Ben Kircher had been in Tintagel, and heard people saying that the body of a young servant girl named Charlotte Dymond had been found on the moor. That same day, in the afternoon, her funeral procession had left Lower Penhale farm, followed largely by strangers. Almost everyone that she had lived with or cared about for the best part of the last seven years was at the Halworthy Inn, for the first day of the magistrates hearing. Those who had assembled sang a hymn before walking behind the horse and the cart carrying Charlotte's body, through fields and lanes towards Trevivian where the Chapmans lived. As the procession stopped to sing another hymn they were joined by Tamson Chapman. She had been so affected by her friend's death that her husband had told her not to go to the churchyard for the burial. But how could she not go to Charlotte's funeral when her body was passing along the lane that ran beside her own kitchen door?

One man turned to look at Tamson as she joined the followers; a stranger. To her distress, he dropped back to walk beside her.
"You knew Charlotte?" he asked. "Did you befriend her?"
"I did sir," she replied, but as a tear rolled down onto her cheek he moved forward again, leaving her alone with her own thoughts and memories. When they

reached the chapel at Tremail another hymn was sung.

Dear friends, behold a helpless child,
Left thoughtless, giddy, young and wild.
In childhood banished from her home,
Nor near her parents durst she come.

The stranger who had spoken to Tamson Chapman was now looking most upset and moved towards her again.

"That hymn," he said, "was that Charlotte? Is that how she felt?"

"That is how it was sir," she replied. "Did you know Charlotte?"

"She was my daughter," he told her. "She was coming home to live with us at Treparrett Post. It was all agreed."

He moved away again and the procession carried on towards the church at Davidstow, where poor Charlotte's body was at last laid to rest in an unmarked grave.

Mrs Hayne, who had been Charlotte's mistress for eighteen months on the farm at Tremail, had come to Davidstow churchyard, ahead of the funeral procession, to be there for the burial of a maid she had been very fond of. When it was over, and the people began to drift
away, she noticed Tamson standing alone and watching a man who was still beside the grave.

"So sad my dear," she said, and Tamson turned towards her, relieved to see someone she recognised. "Do you think Charlotte knew any of those good folk who followed her?"

"Well at least we are here Mrs Hayne," Tamson replied, "and there is a man who told me that Charlotte was his daughter."

She turned then towards the grave, to point him out to her friend, but he was nowhere to be seen.

Saturday 10th August, 1844

That evening Nell Ternouth was sitting alone at her table in the yard of the Halworthy Inn. Her mother had been feeling unwell and had gone home to rest for a while, leaving her to try to sell a trinket or two before the evening was out.

"I would come home with you mother," she'd said, "but we need every penny that we can earn."

"I know girl, I know," her mother had sighed, "business is not so brisk these days. I'll be back to help you pack it all away later."

Business had not been so brisk since they had lost Matthew and the little wood carvings that he had brought for them to sell. But Nell had another reason for wanting to stay behind on her own. She needed to talk with William Northam. There were some 'regulars' out in the yard who she knew well enough, and she asked them to watch her table.

"Will you make sure that no one steals from me?" she begged the group of old men who were sitting beside her, and when they agreed she made her way inside the inn. Hearing William's voice, she walked towards him and stood waiting patiently until he had finished his conversation with a customer.

"Nell dear," he said, noticing her beside him, "are you wanting to talk to me?"

"I have heard," she replied, "that Matthew Weeks is to hang this Friday for the murder of poor Charlotte Dymond. There has been a lot said, but no two stories are the same and my mother refuses to speak of it with me. All she will say is that I have had a lucky escape. You were there Mr Northam, at the trial. Will you tell me what you know? You see, Matthew was very kind to me."

"I know that you were fond of him Nell. Sit down here with me and I'll tell you how this sad business came about. I was there, as I expect you know, when the moor was searched, along with John Westlake. Poor Charlotte had been missing nine days when we set off from Penhale farm with John Peter and his servant John Stevens. Matthew had walked out two days before and not come back. He had been seen going out on the moor with a woman, on that Sunday, 14th April, but he denied it; said that he came up here to Halworthy. No one came forward though, to say that they'd seen him anywhere other than on the moor. Charlotte had been wearing pattens, to protect her shoes, and when I saw patten prints in the lane from the farm and further out on the moor, I measured them with a stick. When we reached the Britannia Inn, near the edge of the moor, John Peter went home and Humphrey Vosper, the landlord, took his place. Others joined us as we followed patten prints towards Roughtor Ford. Simon Baker was there. He keeps a beer shop at Trevalga, and knew Charlotte from a little girl. I found a boot print near to a patten print and measured that with my stick. Simon moved away from the main group of searchers and I followed him, along the right bank of the river Alan until he reached a place where he could see down to a little cove beside the water, and there he saw Charlotte's body. There were no signs of a struggle, but there were some broken beads behind her on the bank."

Nell gasped. She was looking so distressed that he reached out and took her hand in his.
"Coral beads?" she asked. "A little coral necklace?"
"Why yes Nell," he said to her. "How do you know that?"

"I sold him that necklace," she said. "He gave it to Charlotte as a token when they first kept company together. Oh, Mr Northam, I have been so afraid that we started all of this; my mother and myself. He asked us you see, to tell him what John Westlake was saying about him and Charlotte. Mother told him, in the middle of March, that she'd heard as how Charlotte preferred another man; a Thomas Prout. He was so upset by it that he left us, straight away. Were we the cause of this dreadful murder Mr Northam?"

"Dear girl, you mustn't blame yourself! Matthew would have discovered that without your help!"

He fetched her a drink to calm her. "Would you like me to stop now? Have you heard enough?"

"No Mr Northam. I must know the rest."

"Well the beads were given to Mary Westlake when she came with the cart to collect the body. We had to wait there four hours for a surgeon to come, and it was then we found more patten and boot marks, several yards away from the body. The boot marks were clear; best boots, not nailed all over like work boots. I took their measure on my stick before we went back with Charlotte's body to the farm.

The next day there was an inquest in the barn. Mrs Peter had found Matthew's shirt with blood spots on it, though he had killed a pig in the week, and there was no knowing how that blood had got on the shirt.

"He had nose bleeds," Nell said. "I know that. It could have been his own blood."

William nodded. "There were two more witnesses who saw a couple on the moor. William Gard, a preacher, but he was too far away to know them. And a farmer, Richard Pethick from Advent, but he couldn't see the woman's face as she kept an umbrella over her head, and he didn't know Matthew.

Tom Prout told that he was to meet Charlotte at the chapel that evening. There were other things; a letter that was never found and some money of Charlotte's, but it was John Stevens' evidence that took the case onto the magistrates. He said he'd seen Matthew sharpening a razor, and also that he'd bought a knife from a local vendor. The inquest jury decided that the case should go before the magistrate, but no one knew where Matthew had gone."

"One of the constables, who attended the inquest, John Bennett, lives in the next parish beside Lezant, where Matthew's mother lives. He knew the family and he went straight there in his own horse-drawn gig. 'Twas local knowledge that Matthew often visited the Stevens family at Coads Green, who lived close by to his mother'. John Bennett called in on them and found that Matthew had been there, and stayed there with them for six hours on the day that he disappeared from the farm. Elizabeth Stevens, the daughter, told that he'd had a little black handbag in his pocket; very like the one that Charlotte had walked out with on the day she disappeared. The constable knew that Matthew had a sister in Plymouth, so he made his way to Saltash and took the boat across the river Tamar."

"Did Matthew not go to his mother's then?" Nell asked.

"No one mentioned that," William told her, "but Bennett knew that this sister was married and living near to Plymouth Hoe. He had a description of Matthew and when he found him he was walking on the Hoe with his sister and brother-in-law. It was said that Matthew had plans to go to Guernsey or Jersey, but that he had delayed when he found his sister heavy with child."

"So he might have got away?" Nell said, "if he had not been so concerned for his sister."

"He might well have my dear, but even on the day of the trial at the assize court, I thought that he would walk away a free man. By that time there was very little evidence against him, very little. Constable Bennett had searched him on the way back from Plymouth and found a pair of women's gloves in his pockets. They were thought to be Charlotte's, but later on there was some doubt about that. And Bennett questioned him, though he had no business doing it; asked him if he had murdered Charlotte with a pair of fleams. At the magistrates hearing, Bennett said that Matthew had replied 'I did not'. But later in court at Bodmin, Bennett said that Matthew had told him 'not with that'. There was confusion as well when the constable accused him of saying that he thought he would be safe in Plymouth, or that he wouldn't be safe in Plymouth; Bennett couldn't remember. Matthew spoke out then and denied saying it at all. He'd gone there he said, just to see the place, and that he planned to return to Penhale farm."

Nell interrupted him suddenly. "Matthew was here at the inn when he came before the magistrates. My mother kept me away."

"They wouldn't have let you see him my dear, but he was here, chained to the bar in the parlour. Charlotte's body had been found and Mrs Peter had to prosecute, but I could tell she wasn't happy about it. She'd thought highly of Matthew."

"What of the boot prints that you found Mr Northam?"

"Well they seemed to match with the best boots that Matthew was wearing. The measurement of the right boot print was too short, but since the toe turned up on that boot, with Matthew being so lame, it was thought that the print wouldn't be as long as the boot. The main reason that the case went to the assize court though Nell, was based on John Stevens' evidence. The knife he'd seen Matthew buy, and another knife he'd seen him with when he killed the pig. At that point you see, no one had been able to swear that it was Matthew and Charlotte they'd seen on the moor that day, and no weapon had been found."

"But you said Matthew had been seen going out on the moor with a woman?" Nell had taken in every word that William had spoken.

"Isaac Cory couldn't swear to Charlotte. And he only knew Matthew by his limp. His sight's not good Nell, we all know that. He stuck by his story of knowing it was Matthew though, probably because he was afraid it could have been his nephew Tom Prout out there on the moor with Charlotte. Tom was limping bad back then. He'd fallen off a farm cart so Mrs Peter told me."

"So Tom is his nephew and Isaac was shielding him?" William Northam nodded. He continued.

"It was Isaac who went on the moor with his wife and found Charlotte's clothes buried in a turf pit. That was after the poor girl's funeral. A lot of blood was also found that day by Constable Rickard buried near the murder spot. As I was saying Nell, when the case was heard last week, on the 2nd, in the assize court, it appeared that there was no positive evidence against Matthew. The boot print evidence was weak. John Stevens had thought better of his statement about the knives, saying that when he'd looked in Matthew's bedroom box, he'd only found a pair of new braces, not a knife. And the knife that killed the pig, he was now saying belonged to John Chapman, the butcher! The prosecution was relying on Richard Pethick. He'd made a new statement, saying that he hadn't been asked to swear positively that it was Matthew on the moor. He was now prepared to do that in the assize court. When he went into the witness box he said, again, that he believed that Matthew was the man on the moor. It wasn't enough you see Nell, not positive enough. But then, just as his cross-examination was about to close, he said that he would swear that the prisoner was the man on the moor, and that it was beyond belief! It was all over then for Matthew. In the eyes of the court he was guilty. When the judge sentenced him, he collapsed and had to be carried, unconscious, to the prison van."

William's wife came over to them, smiling. "Nell's mother is out in the yard, packing up their things. She's asking for you Nell."
"Thank you Mr Northam," the girl said as she stood up to leave. "Now I know the real story, but I'll never believe that Matthew killed Charlotte."
"You're not the only one with doubts my dear," he said kindly. "I hear it all the time."

Matthew was surprised to receive so many visitors in his cell at Bodmin Gaol on Saturday August 10th. His execution was arranged for the following Monday and he had spent much of the past three months in the company of the Reverend Kendall, the prison chaplain. On this day though, he was allowed to meet

241

with any friends or family who wished to see him before the execution. Over the past few weeks, he had been collapsing and passing into a state of unconsciousness, almost on a daily basis. It had been expected, and he had hoped, that he would die before he could be hanged, but he had survived, and now he was grateful that he was able to meet, for this one last time, with at least some of the people who had meant so much to him in his short lifetime. His three brothers arrived together, and at first it was awkward, meeting under such awful circumstances. But then he told them of his illness and how it often caused him to pass out and wake up in a daze.

"Strange that you should say that Matthew," his brother John said, "that happens to me most days, but I thought it was the drink that caused it."

They all started laughing then, and were easy together again.

Over the past months he had heard nothing of his mother and it greatly upset him to hear that she had been deeply distressed by his terrible plight and was now at times still quite distraught. His sister Eliza was the only one of the family still living at home with their mother.

"I don't know how mother would have got through this," his brother William had said, "if she didn't have Eliza there. But we're helping her Matthew," he assured him, seeing his brother's anguished face, "and the girls, and uncle Richard; we're all helping her."

Parting company with them was almost unbearable; as it was with all of those who visited him that day. He was much cheered that Will came to see him, and surprised to receive a visit from Mr Hayne, who spoke mostly of Thomasine and the twins; and shook his hand before leaving. His greatest shock was on seeing John Peter enter his cell, followed by his mistress. They had been witnesses against him but he found that he had no ill feelings for them. John was unchanged, affable but speaking with little thought of their new maid Sarah and a farm servant, George. John Stevens, he said, was still with them. His mistress, though, was silent and most upset, moving Matthew to console her.

"You will have a letter from me mistress," he said. "I have to write a letter, to say that I forgive you, and the master, for what you had to do and say against me. I've been told it's expected of me to write this letter, but I beg you to believe my words mistress. I do forgive you. You only told the court the truth."

She didn't reply, but sat with her head bowed.

"I left my toolbox unlocked when I went to Plymouth," he said to John Peter. "I want you to have the tools from it; they'll come in useful. And mistress, there are three little wood carvings in the box. I'd like you to have them."

She nodded, but said nothing.

John Peter left first, but his mistress seemed reluctant to follow him.

"I didn't kill her mistress," he said. "I didn't kill Charlotte. I was with her on the moor, but I collapsed, and when I woke up she was dead."

"That was all I wanted from you Matthew." She held out her hands to him. "All that badgering was for the truth. I would have known the truth."

On Sunday, August 11th, a service was held in the prison chapel and Matthew attended to take the holy sacrament. Afterwards, he returned to his cell to wait for the chaplain, Mr Kendall, who was to write down his confession and his letters to the Peters and to his mother.

"How can I write a confession when I am not guilty?" Matthew asked the reverend when he arrived.

"You have to write a confession Matthew," the Reverend Kendall said. "It has to be written and posted on the gates of the gaol after your execution, to save the consciences of all those who were witnesses against you in the courtroom."

"Then I have to tell my mother, in her letter, that I am not guilty. She has to know that I am still saying this."

"I have to write these things down for you Matthew, since you cannot do it for yourself. How can I send a letter to your mother which says that you are not guilty, and then take down your confession, which will state that you are guilty?"

They had spoken of this before, and as they sat down to write to his mother, Matthew was at a loss for words.

"You have told me Matthew, that your father died some time ago. Was that the truth?" the reverend asked.

"Nine years ago Mr Kendall," Matthew replied.

"This letter will have to be read out to your mother? I assume she cannot read Matthew, but is she an intelligent woman?"

"She is Mr Kendall. My mother's very knowing."

"Then how would it be if we start your letter? 'My dear father and mother'."

Early September 1844

He found Unity sitting in the hedge behind their tent, flirting with young Danny, his cousin's boy. She was wearing a pretty blouse and skirt; silver bangles on her wrists. Ben sat down beside them.

"I'm leaving soon," he said. "You'll be alright though? I'll be back the day after tomorrow."

She nodded, taking Danny's hand in hers.

"Are you going to the farm father?"

"Next time my love. We'll go together then and take a cart; bring back whatever you want to keep. This trip is just to make arrangements to sell the farm and the horses."

They were camping near Clovelly in Devon with their family. Much to his relief, there were no plans to return to Cornwall this year. They were leaving within the month, to slowly make their way up to Scotland. This journey to Trebarwith was purely business. When Ben rode away, they were still sitting in the hedge, holding hands and looking into each other's eyes. Unity was happy and he realised that the traveller's way of life was in her blood. She had loved the farm, but there she had lost her girlish ways, working with the men as if she was one of them, wearing those boy's clothes and heavy boots; cutting her hair short. He had more plans though, to buy another farm, perhaps in Scotland on the coast and start again. She would have to make a decision then, settle down with him, or stay with the family, travelling around the country with Danny.

It was early September now and only three weeks had passed since the hanging. It might have all been quite different if he hadn't been ill on that Sunday, too ill to meet Charlotte on the moor. He'd suffered for several days with stomach pains, mostly after his meals, but on that day, after dinner, the pain had been crippling. He'd taken to his bed and Unity had given him a sleeping draught. She'd promised to ride to Roughtor Ford and see if Charlotte had come out to meet him. *'Be there by five o'clock'* he'd told her. *'If she's not there then, we'll know she's made other plans and won't be coming to stay with us'.*

When he'd woken late in the evening, she had already returned, but without Charlotte. *'I was there before five o'clock and waited for the best part of an hour,'* she'd said. *'It was misty, and at times I could see for miles and there was no sign of her.'* If he'd been able to go there that day, he would have waited longer. He might have been able to save her. He was hoping now that he wouldn't hear anything of Matthew Weeks on this brief visit back to Cornwall. The farm had been a dream that he had lived for a short while. He had even thought, that one day in the future, when Unity took a husband, he would find himself a good woman and marry again. There had only been one other love in his life since the loss of his wife and infant son. Several years had passed by before he'd met Sophie, the daughter of a farmer who'd bought horses from him, when his family made camp for a few months near the New Forest. Her own family had been travellers who had settled there before she'd been born, and he'd soon fallen for her lovely face and carefree ways. He had courted her, taken her to meet his family, and his daughter had been affectionate towards his new love from the start. Sophie and Unity had spent many hours riding their horses in the neighbouring countryside together, until the day that Romany had seemed quite lame and

Sophie had ridden off on her own to exercise her horse in the forest. She hadn't returned, and Unity had taken his horse, hoping to find her.

'We always take the same paths,' she'd said. *I know where to look father. I'll be back if we need your help.'* She had come back alone, and in tears and told of having found his Sophie on a path they often used. *'She must have fallen father. She's hit her head against a tree, and she's just lying there. I can't rouse her. I think she's dead and her horse must have bolted. I couldn't see him around anywhere.'*

He'd ridden out with her, praying that she was wrong and that Sophie could be saved, but the wound on her head had been so bad that she would never have survived. After that, Unity had been the only girl in his life, until the day that he'd met Charlotte again.

He hadn't planned to go to the farm that day, but when he reached Trebarwith his thoughts were all for the men who had so loyally agreed to run his farm for him while he was away; and for those horses he had so hurriedly left behind. As he rode into the farmyard, he could see two of his farmhands out in the nearest field with a colt. One of them had seen him riding in and held up his hand. They would be back to talk to him before long. He went into the kitchen. Somebody had been looking after the place; it was clean and tidy; Unity's plates and porcelain figures, still spotless on the shelves of the dresser. He would look upstairs; come back down and make himself a drink; see if he could find anything to eat out in the larder. His bedroom was just as he had left it, though his bed had been made. Unity must have made it before she went out riding that day. He went into her room. Her nightclothes were still lying untidily on top of the chest of drawers he had brought back from a farm sale. There was no reason to take anything back to the camp today. They had everything that they needed for now, and he could return with a cart when the place was sold. Charlotte's bonnet cap. He could take that. Pulling open the top drawer he searched around at the back, before taking out the pretty piece of lace that had belonged to his eldest daughter. It had been folded, and as he shook it open a few brightly coloured beads fell to the floor and scattered, before rolling back one by one to nestle together at his feet. Charlotte's beads. He knew them straight away.

'No two of these necklaces are ever fashioned the same,'

she'd told him. He'd laughed. *'There is an unusual cut to the bead.'*

Gathering them up, he sat down on his daughter's bed and wept. At first for Charlotte and Matthew; but then for his infant son and poor carefree Sophie.

Epilogue

"I'm thinking I'll ride over to Roughtor Ford after dinner mother to see that monument they've put up for Charlotte. I'll take the cart if you want to come with me."

"Oh John. I'm not sure I want to see it; though it has to be better than that black flag that's been flying out there ever since they found the poor girl. It's time to let it rest now if you ask me; and instead they've put up some monument that'll bring folk out there to look at it for evermore."

"Well it's too late now mother. There was a lot of money collected for it at that rally they held out there after the murder. They've built it, so we may as well go out and take a look at it."

"All right then son, I'll come with you. I don't suppose you want to go there on your own or you wouldn't have asked me."

They mostly ate their Sunday dinner on their own these days. Sarah Westlake was ailing, and all of Mary's time was taken up caring for her three boisterous youngsters. The servants too, were busy with their own lives.

"That was good mother." John Peter had cleared a plate of his favourite pork and vegetables and pushed it to one side. "Shall we save that apple pie for later? I'll enjoy it better after a bit of a walk."

They reached the ford to see that they weren't alone out there that day. Others had gathered around the tall granite monument by the river, and a few more were bravely climbing Cornwall's second highest tor.

"There's something written on it," John said, and they moved closer to be able to read the words that had been carved into the stone.

"Monument erected by public subscription in memory of Charlotte Dymond who was murdered by Matthew Weeks, Sunday, April 14th, 1844." Phillipa Peter had read it aloud.

"And may God rest both their souls." John Peter said, and several people turned to look at him.

"Amen to that!" Someone spoke from behind them and then Emily Mudge was at their side.

"It's good to see you Phillipa," she said, and the two women hugged each other. They had become friends over time, often meeting when Charlotte had visited Emily at the doctor's house in Bodmin, and more recently, at the market.

"I'll leave you ladies to chinwag. I think I'll take a little walk up on Roughtor." John left the two women sitting together on the cart mulling over old times.

"He didn't do it you know Emily. He told me that he collapsed out here somewhere, and when he came around he found her dead by the river."

"He passed out on my doorstep once," Emily said, "just fainted clean away. I had to get my smelling salts to revive him."

They sat together in this way for more than an hour before Emily suddenly linked her arm through Phillipa's.

"I know I'm being silly my dear, but I feel as though Charlotte and Matthew are right here with us, flying with those buzzards, running with the horses; and she lifted her head to watch two big birds that were circling high above them. Phillipa turned away a little to look for John, and saw a fine white horse just a few feet away, gazing straight towards her. Mesmerized, she gazed back into thoughtful eyes and a gentle face, half dappled with grey. A sure footed brown stallion approached, cantering by, without even a glance in their direction. The white horse moved off then, breaking into a gallop to follow the stallion towards Charlotte's monument, where they both turned behind it; slowing to pick their way carefully down to the river, and out of sight.

"That's enough walking for me today!" John had arrived beside them, hands in his pockets and smiling. "You ready for home then mother? I was up there on that little mountain and I'll swear I could taste your apple pie!"